STAR WARS™
ADVENTURES
Mechanical Mayhem

Facebook: **facebook.com/idwpublishing**
Twitter: **@idwpublishing**
YouTube: **youtube.com/idwpublishing**
Tumblr: **tumblr.idwpublishing.com**
Instagram: **instagram.com/idwpublishing**

ISBN: 978-1-68405-422-0   22 21 20 19   1 2 3 4

COVER ARTIST
CHAD THOMAS

COVER COLORIST
JORDAN BOYD

LETTERER
TOM B. LONG

SERIES ASSISTANT EDITOR
ELIZABETH BREI

SERIES EDITORS
DENTON J. TIPTON
& BOBBY CURNOW

COLLECTION EDITORS
JUSTIN EISINGER
& ALONZO SIMON

COLLECTION DESIGNER
CLYDE GRAPA

PUBLISHER
GREG GOLDSTEIN

Originally published as STAR WARS ADVENTURES issues #9, 12,
and 13.

Greg Goldstein, President and Publisher
John Barber, Editor-In-Chief
Robbie Robbins, EVP/Sr. Art Director
Cara Morrison, Chief Financial Officer
Matt Ruzicka, Chief Accounting Officer
Anita Frazier, SVP of Sales and Marketing
David Hedgecock, Associate Publisher
Jerry Bennington, VP of New Product Development
Lorelei Bunjes, VP of Digital Services
Justin Eisinger, Editorial Director, Graphic Novels & Collections
Eric Moss, Senior Director, Licensing and Business Development

Ted Adams, IDW Founder

Lucasfilm Credits:
Senior Editor: Robert Simpson
Editorial Assistant: Nicholas Martino
Creative Director: Michael Siglain
Story Group: James Waugh, Leland Chee,
Pablo Hidalgo, Matt Martin

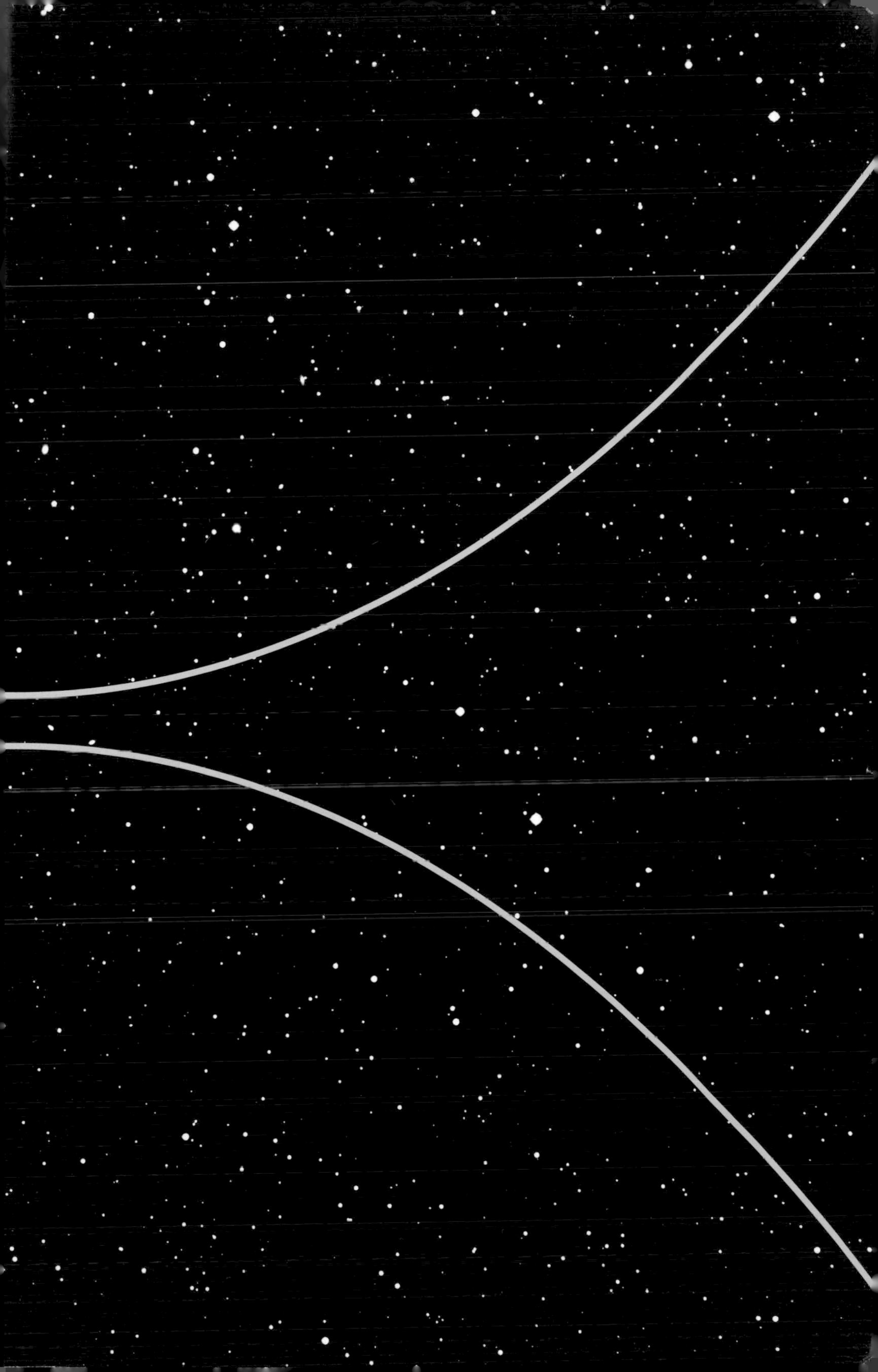

STAR WARS ADVENTURES

Trouble Again

WRITER
JOHN BARBER
ARTIST
CHAD THOMAS
COLORIST
MATT HERMS

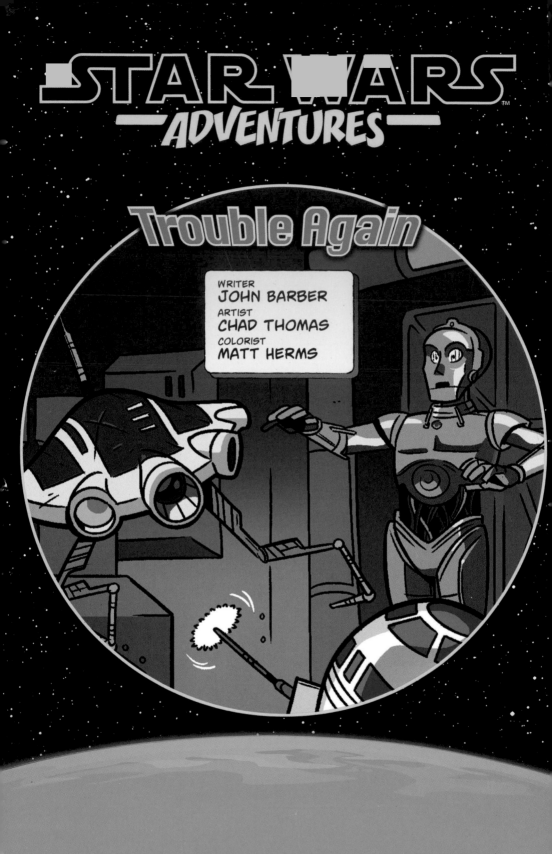

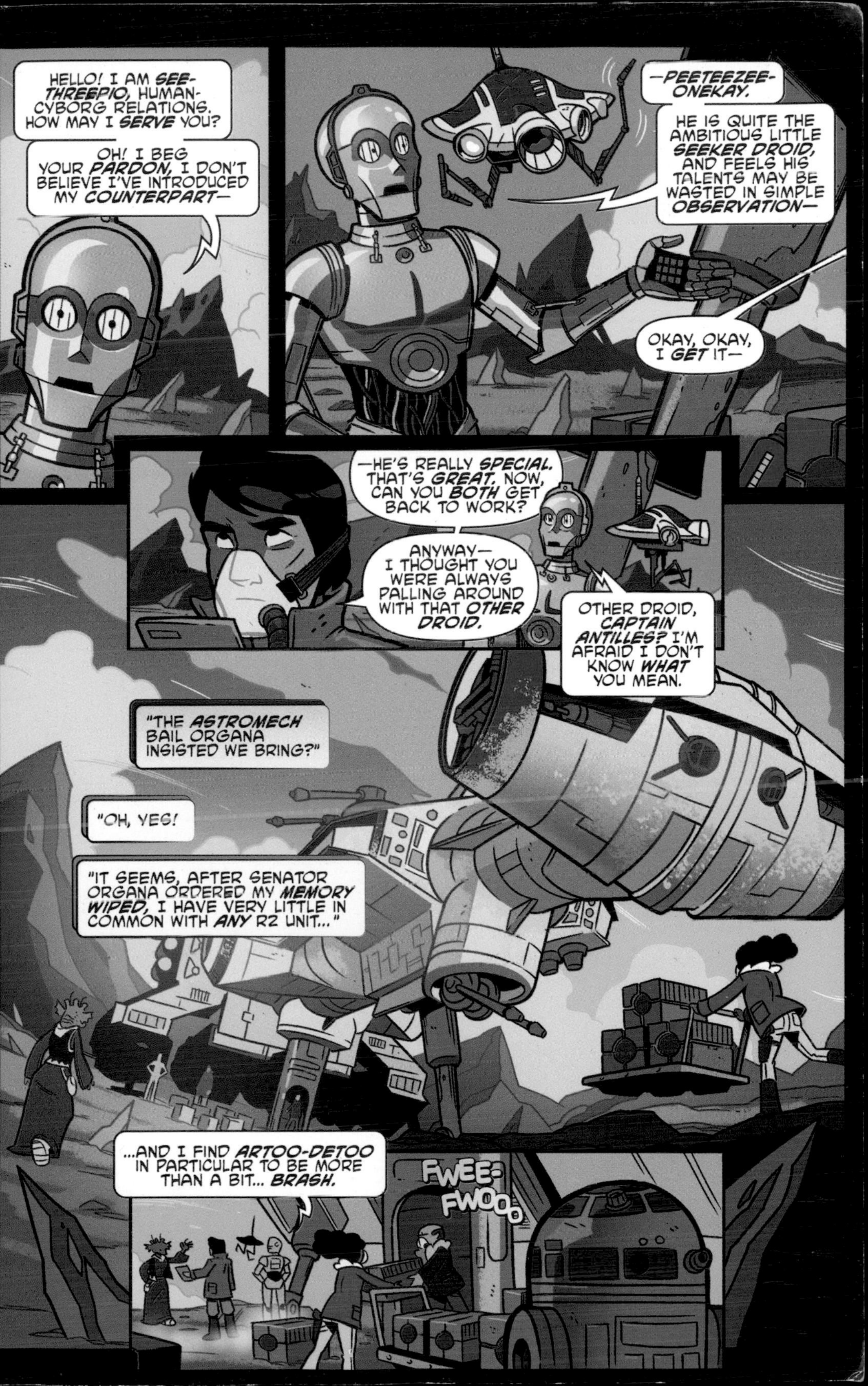

HELLO! I AM SEE-THREEPIO, HUMAN-CYBORG RELATIONS. HOW MAY I SERVE YOU?
OH! I BEG YOUR PARDON, I DON'T BELIEVE I'VE INTRODUCED MY COUNTERPART—
—PEETEEZEE-ONEKAY.
HE IS QUITE THE AMBITIOUS LITTLE SEEKER DROID, AND FEELS HIS TALENTS MAY BE WASTED IN SIMPLE OBSERVATION—
OKAY, OKAY, I GET IT—
—HE'S REALLY SPECIAL. THAT'S GREAT. NOW, CAN YOU BOTH GET BACK TO WORK?
ANYWAY— I THOUGHT YOU WERE ALWAYS PALLING AROUND WITH THAT OTHER DROID.
OTHER DROID, CAPTAIN ANTILLES? I'M AFRAID I DON'T KNOW WHAT YOU MEAN.
"THE ASTROMECH BAIL ORGANA INSISTED WE BRING?"
"OH, YES!
"IT SEEMS, AFTER SENATOR ORGANA ORDERED MY MEMORY WIPED, I HAVE VERY LITTLE IN COMMON WITH ANY R2 UNIT..."
...AND I FIND ARTOO-DETOO IN PARTICULAR TO BE MORE THAN A BIT... BRASH.
FWEE-FWOOO

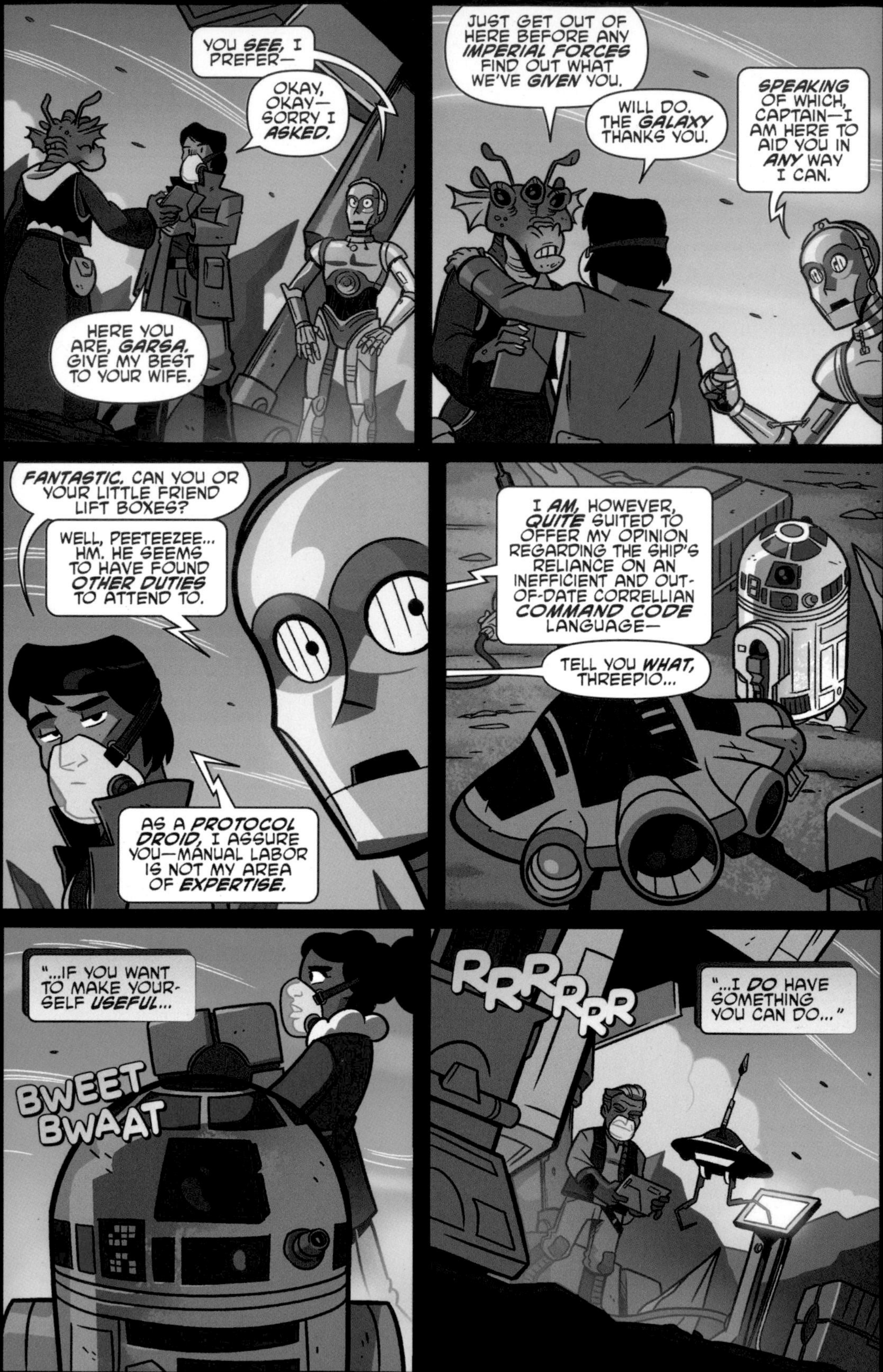
YOU SEE, I PREFER—
OKAY, OKAY—SORRY I ASKED.
HERE YOU ARE, GARSA. GIVE MY BEST TO YOUR WIFE.
JUST GET OUT OF HERE BEFORE ANY IMPERIAL FORCES FIND OUT WHAT WE'VE GIVEN YOU.
WILL DO. THE GALAXY THANKS YOU.
SPEAKING OF WHICH, CAPTAIN—I AM HERE TO AID YOU IN ANY WAY I CAN.
FANTASTIC. CAN YOU OR YOUR LITTLE FRIEND LIFT BOXES?
WELL, PEETEEZEE... HM. HE SEEMS TO HAVE FOUND OTHER DUTIES TO ATTEND TO.
AS A PROTOCOL DROID, I ASSURE YOU—MANUAL LABOR IS NOT MY AREA OF EXPERTISE.
I AM, HOWEVER, QUITE SUITED TO OFFER MY OPINION REGARDING THE SHIP'S RELIANCE ON AN INEFFICIENT AND OUT-OF-DATE CORRELLIAN COMMAND CODE LANGUAGE—
TELL YOU WHAT, THREEPIO...
"...IF YOU WANT TO MAKE YOURSELF USEFUL...
BWEET BWAAT
RRRRRR
"...I DO HAVE SOMETHING YOU CAN DO..."

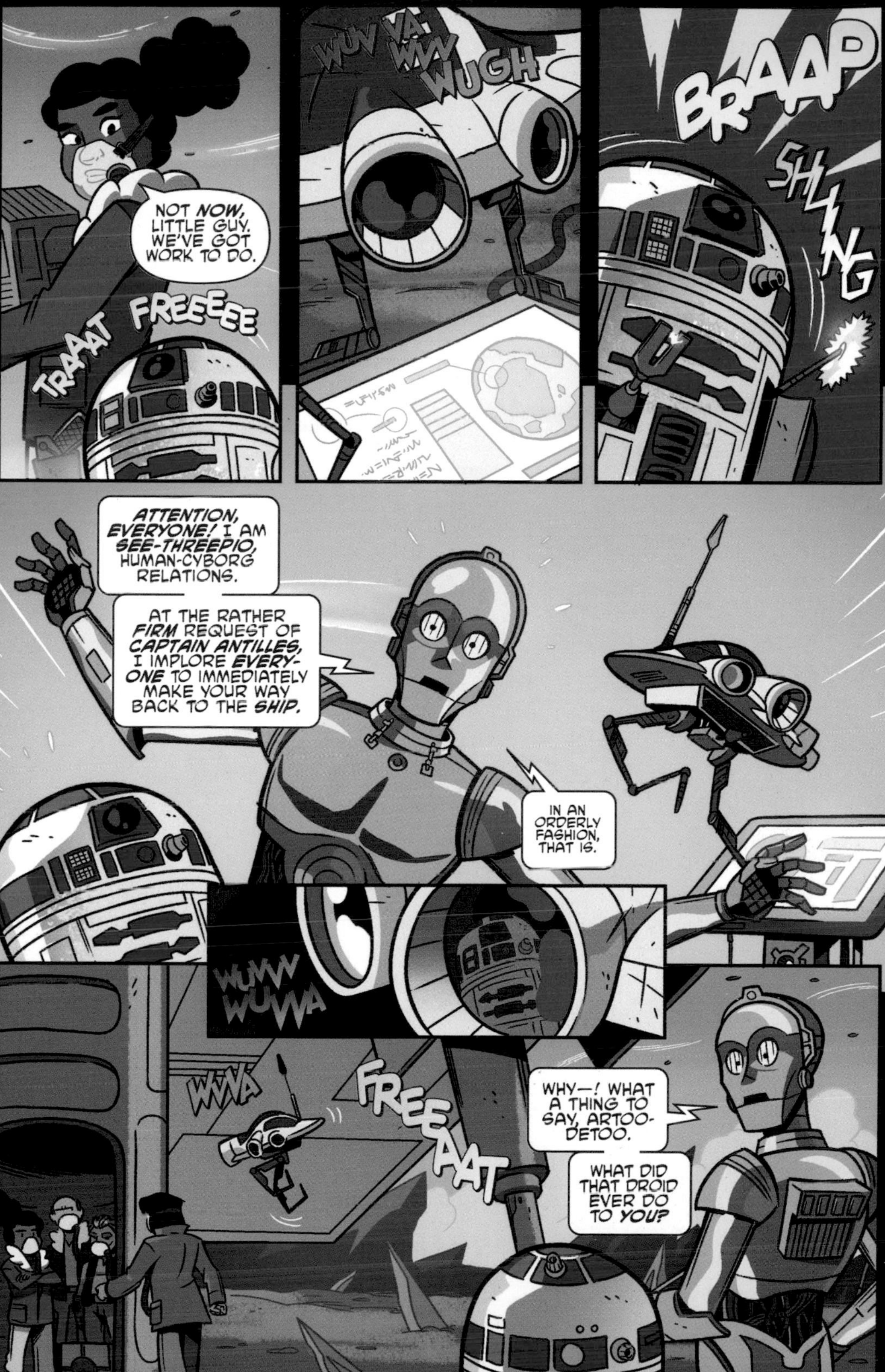
NOT NOW, LITTLE GUY. WE'VE GOT WORK TO DO.
TRAAAT FREEEEE
WUV VA WVV WUGH
BRAAAP
SHING
ATTENTION, EVERYONE! I AM SEE-THREEPIO, HUMAN-CYBORG RELATIONS.
AT THE RATHER FIRM REQUEST OF CAPTAIN ANTILLES, I IMPLORE EVERYONE TO IMMEDIATELY MAKE YOUR WAY BACK TO THE SHIP.
IN AN ORDERLY FASHION, THAT IS.
WUVV WUVVA
WVVA
FREEEAAT
WHY—! WHAT A THING TO SAY, ARTOO-DETOO.
WHAT DID THAT DROID EVER DO TO YOU?

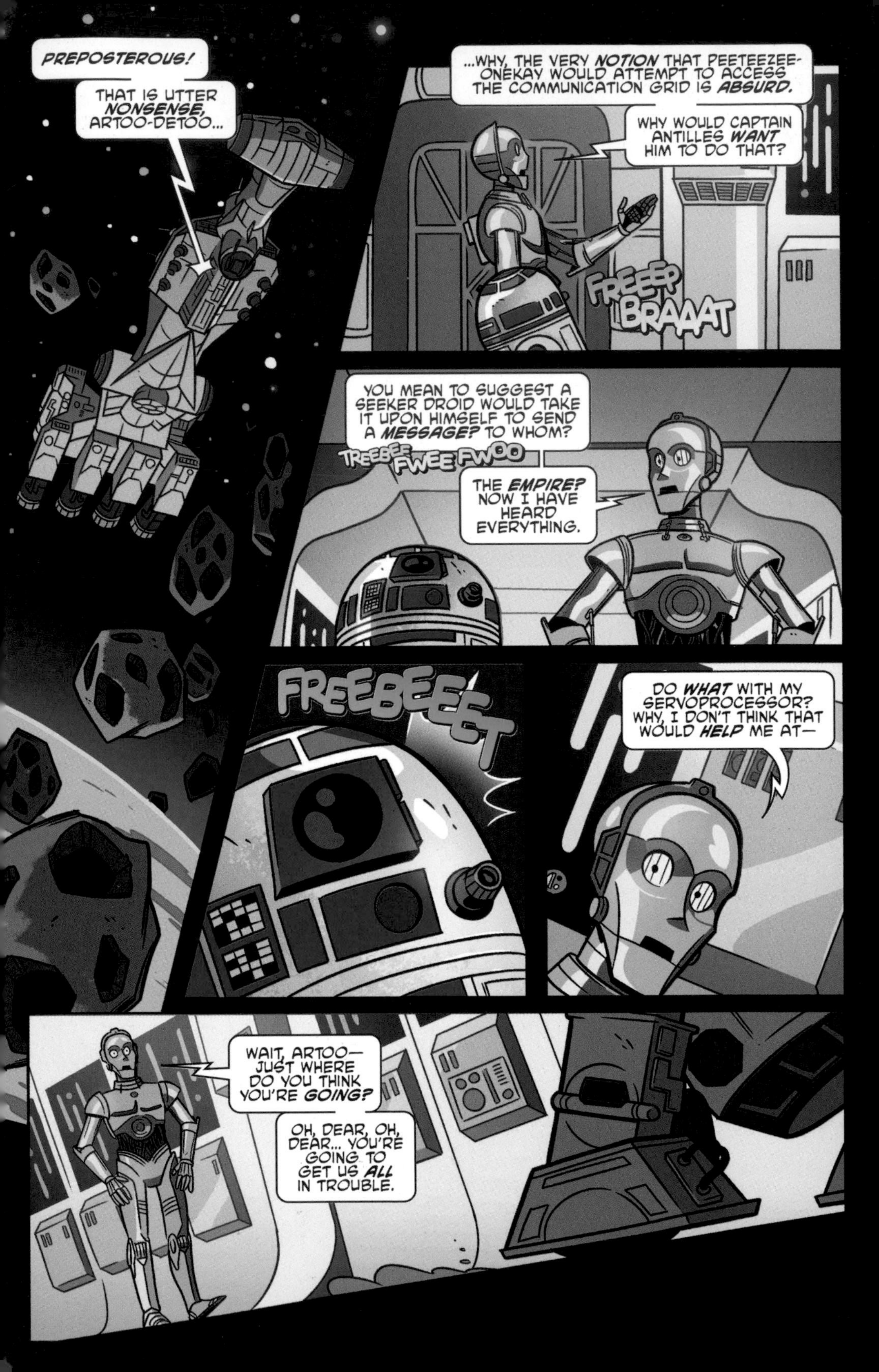
PREPOSTEROUS!
THAT IS UTTER NONSENSE, ARTOO-DETOO...
...WHY, THE VERY NOTION THAT PEETEEZEE-ONEKAY WOULD ATTEMPT TO ACCESS THE COMMUNICATION GRID IS ABSURD.
WHY WOULD CAPTAIN ANTILLES WANT HIM TO DO THAT?
FREEEP BRAAAT
YOU MEAN TO SUGGEST A SEEKER DROID WOULD TAKE IT UPON HIMSELF TO SEND A MESSAGE? TO WHOM?
TREEBEEP FWEE FWOO
THE EMPIRE? NOW I HAVE HEARD EVERYTHING.
FREEBEEEEET
DO WHAT WITH MY SERVOPROCESSOR? WHY, I DON'T THINK THAT WOULD HELP ME AT—
WAIT, ARTOO— JUST WHERE DO YOU THINK YOU'RE GOING?
OH, DEAR, OH, DEAR... YOU'RE GOING TO GET US ALL IN TROUBLE.

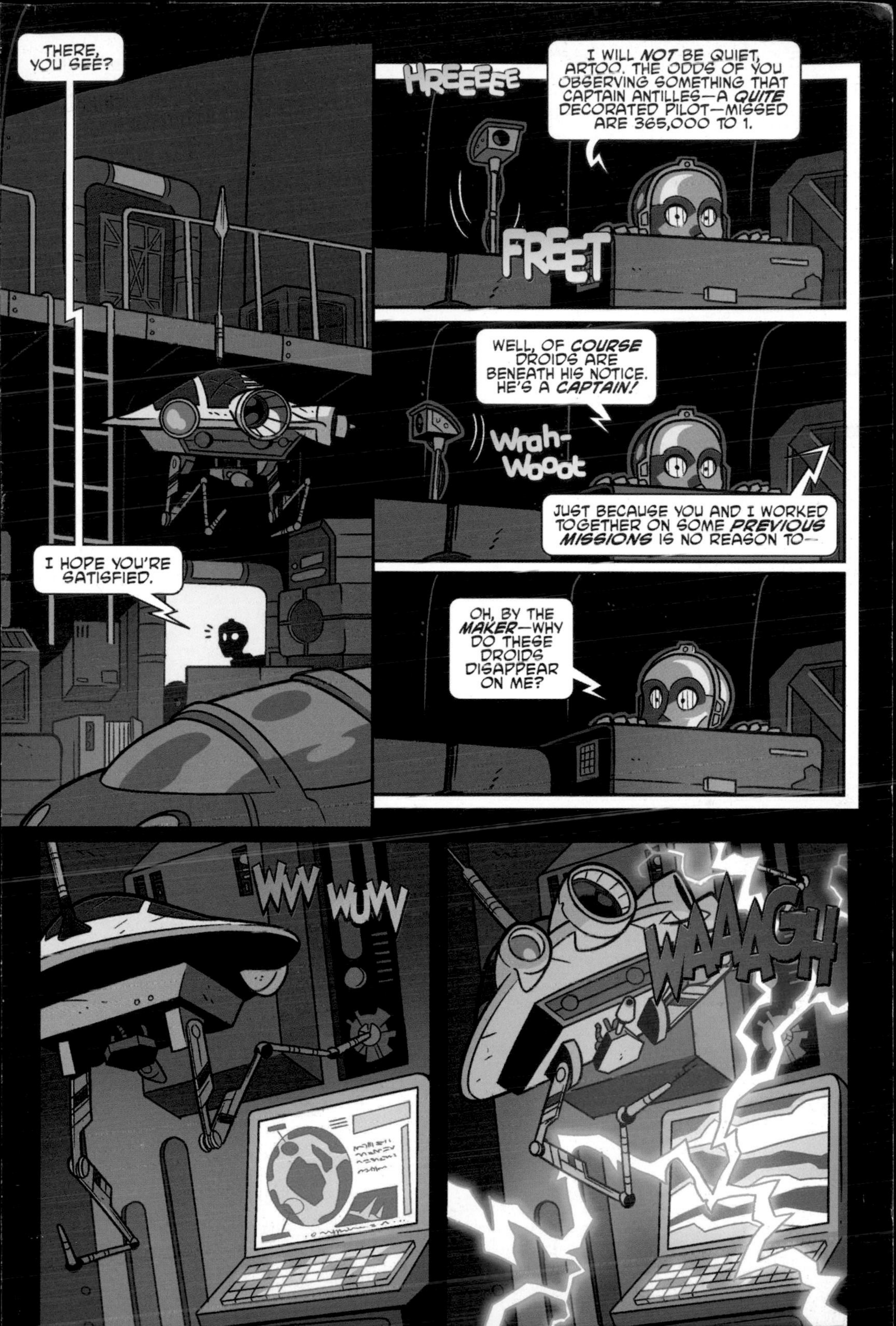

THERE, YOU SEE?
HREEEEEE
I WILL NOT BE QUIET, ARTOO. THE ODDS OF YOU OBSERVING SOMETHING THAT CAPTAIN ANTILLES—A QUITE DECORATED PILOT—MISSED ARE 365,000 TO 1.
FREET
WELL, OF COURSE DROIDS ARE BENEATH HIS NOTICE. HE'S A CAPTAIN!
Wrah-Wooot
JUST BECAUSE YOU AND I WORKED TOGETHER ON SOME PREVIOUS MISSIONS IS NO REASON TO—
I HOPE YOU'RE SATISFIED.
OH, BY THE MAKER—WHY DO THESE DROIDS DISAPPEAR ON ME?
WVV WUVV
WAAAGH

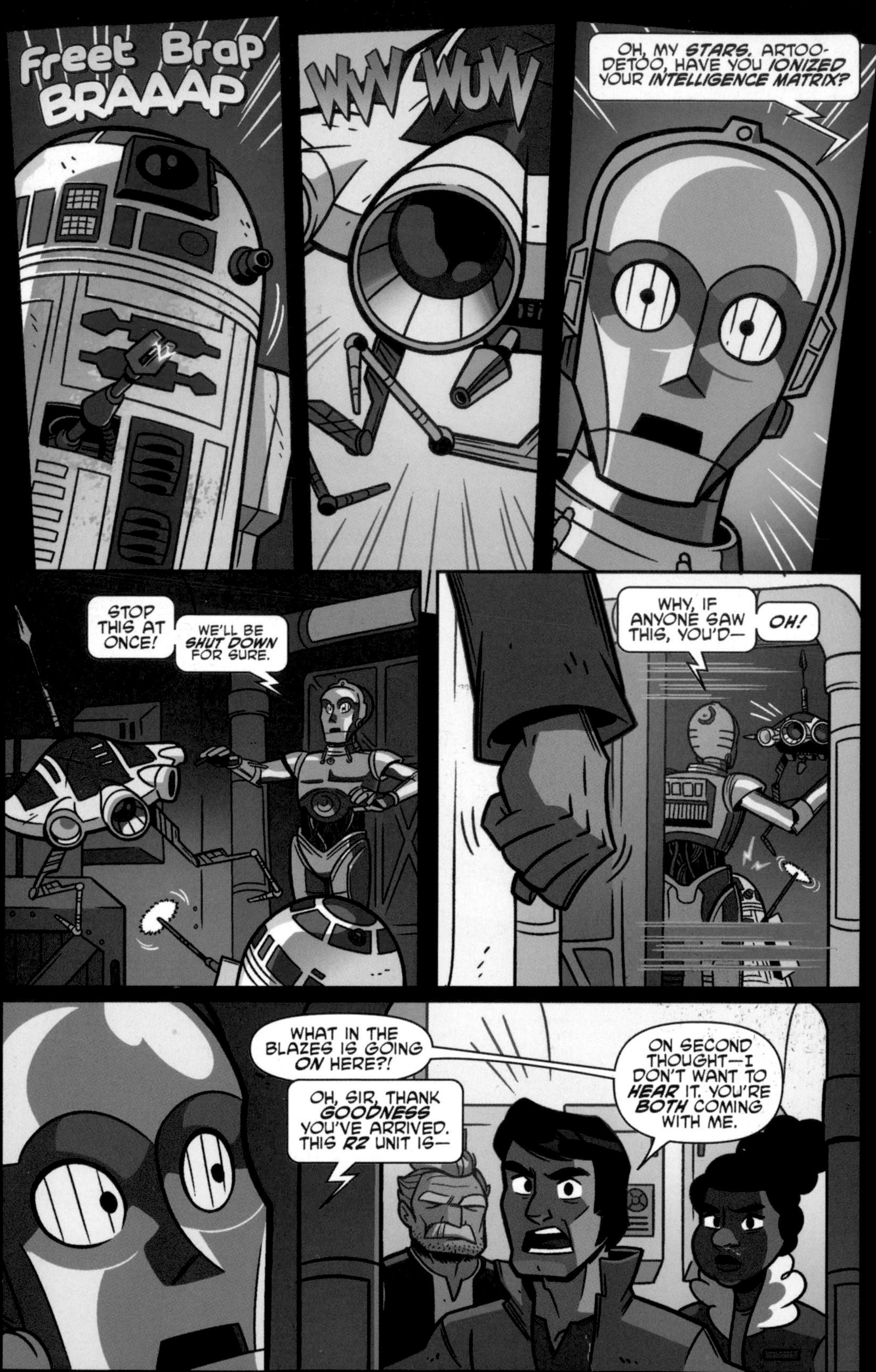

Freet Brap BRAAAP
WUV WUV
OH, MY STARS, ARTOO-DETOO, HAVE YOU IONIZED YOUR INTELLIGENCE MATRIX?
STOP THIS AT ONCE!
WE'LL BE SHUT DOWN FOR SURE.
WHY, IF ANYONE SAW THIS, YOU'D—
OH!
WHAT IN THE BLAZES IS GOING ON HERE?!
OH, SIR, THANK GOODNESS YOU'VE ARRIVED. THIS R2 UNIT IS—
ON SECOND THOUGHT—I DON'T WANT TO HEAR IT. YOU'RE BOTH COMING WITH ME.

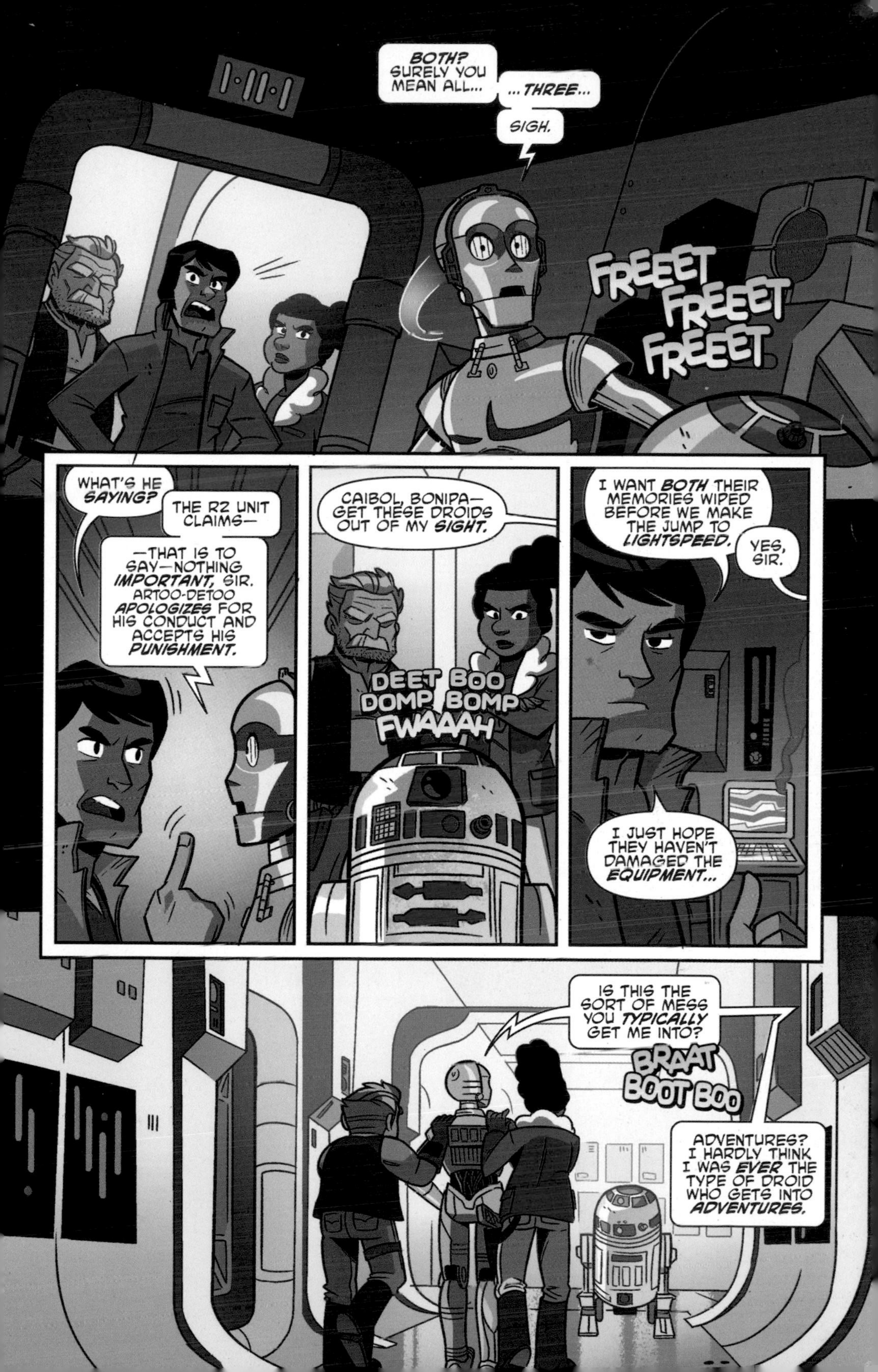
BOTH? SURELY YOU MEAN ALL...
...THREE...
SIGH.
FREEET FREEET FREEET
WHAT'S HE SAYING?
THE R2 UNIT CLAIMS—
—THAT IS TO SAY—NOTHING IMPORTANT, SIR. ARTOO-DETOO APOLOGIZES FOR HIS CONDUCT AND ACCEPTS HIS PUNISHMENT.
CAIBOL, BONIPA—GET THESE DROIDS OUT OF MY SIGHT.
DEET BOO DOMP BOMP FWAAAH
I WANT BOTH THEIR MEMORIES WIPED BEFORE WE MAKE THE JUMP TO LIGHTSPEED.
YES, SIR.
I JUST HOPE THEY HAVEN'T DAMAGED THE EQUIPMENT...
IS THIS THE SORT OF MESS YOU TYPICALLY GET ME INTO?
BRAAT BOOT BOO
ADVENTURES? I HARDLY THINK I WAS EVER THE TYPE OF DROID WHO GETS INTO ADVENTURES.

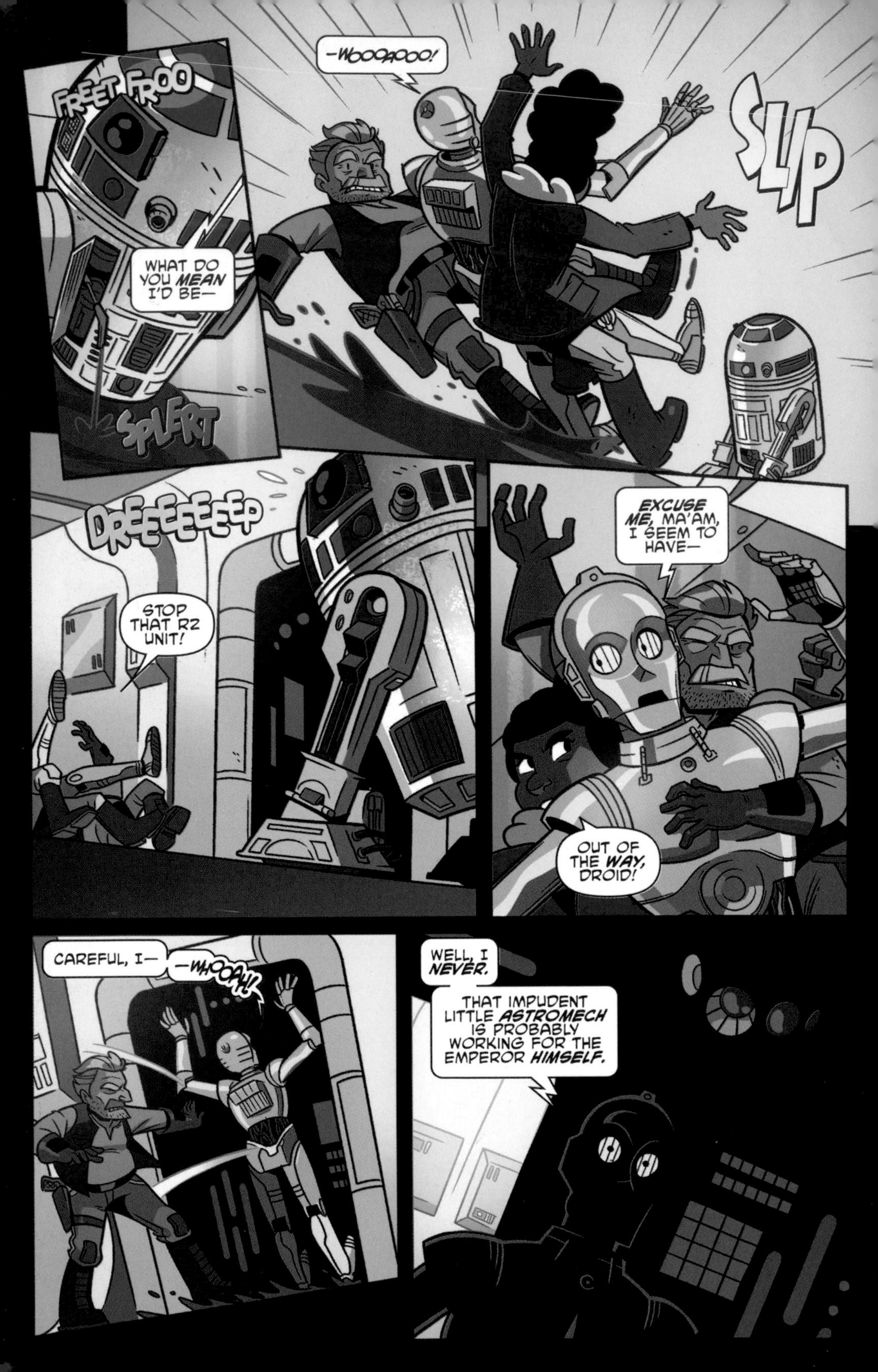
FREET FROO
SPLERT
WHAT DO YOU *MEAN* I'D BE—
—WOOOAOOO!
SLIP
DREEEEEEEP
STOP THAT R2 UNIT!
EXCUSE ME, MA'AM, I SEEM TO HAVE—
OUT OF THE *WAY,* DROID!
CAREFUL, I—
—WHOOAH!
WELL, I *NEVER.*
THAT IMPUDENT LITTLE *ASTROMECH* IS PROBABLY WORKING FOR THE EMPEROR *HIMSELF.*

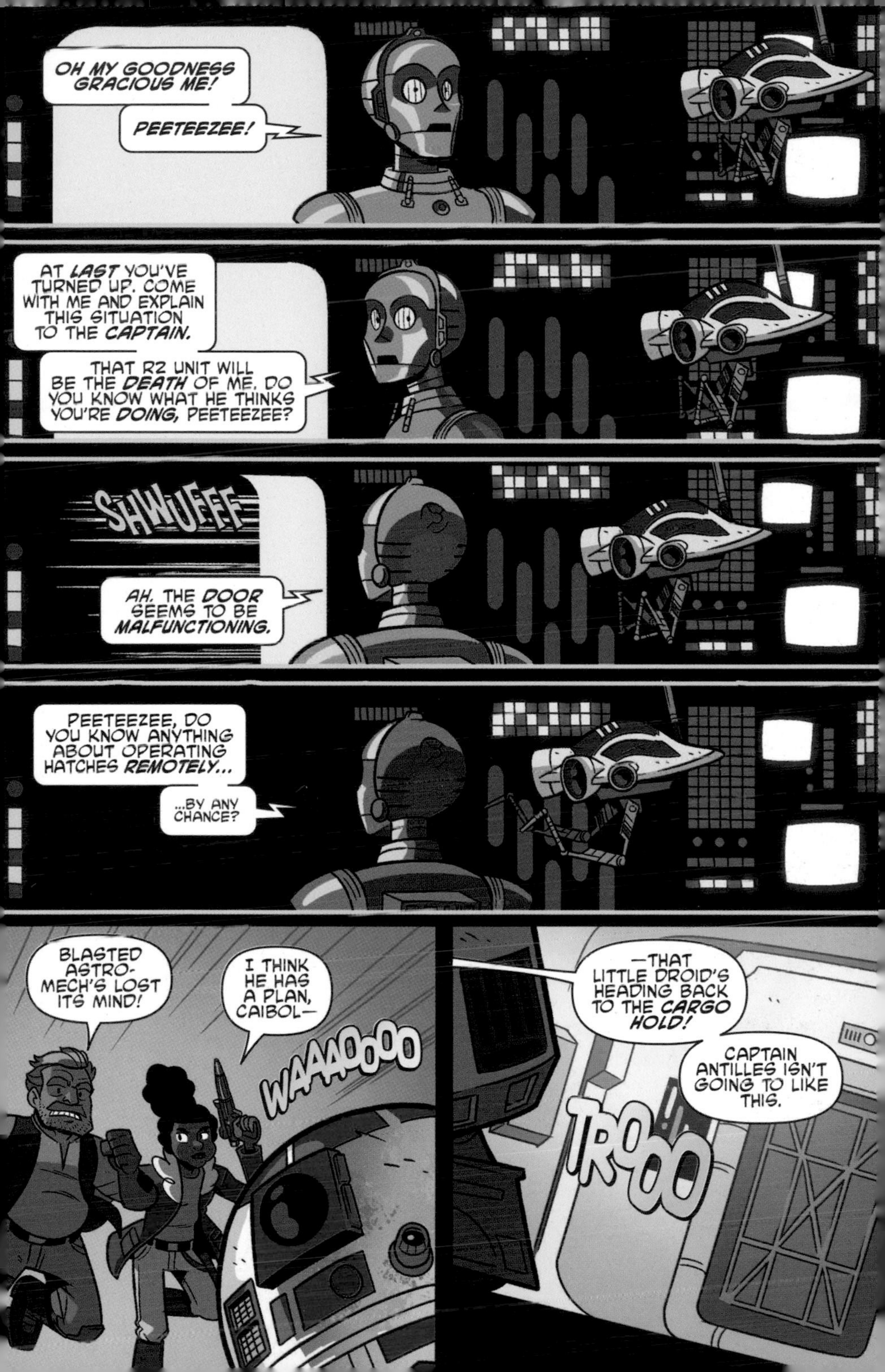
OH MY GOODNESS GRACIOUS ME!
PEETEEZEE!
AT LAST YOU'VE TURNED UP. COME WITH ME AND EXPLAIN THIS SITUATION TO THE CAPTAIN.
THAT R2 UNIT WILL BE THE DEATH OF ME. DO YOU KNOW WHAT HE THINKS YOU'RE DOING, PEETEEZEE?
SHWUFFF
AH. THE DOOR SEEMS TO BE MALFUNCTIONING.
PEETEEZEE, DO YOU KNOW ANYTHING ABOUT OPERATING HATCHES REMOTELY...
...BY ANY CHANCE?
BLASTED ASTRO-MECH'S LOST ITS MIND!
I THINK HE HAS A PLAN, CAIBOL—
WAAAOOOO
—THAT LITTLE DROID'S HEADING BACK TO THE CARGO HOLD!
CAPTAIN ANTILLES ISN'T GOING TO LIKE THIS.
TROOO

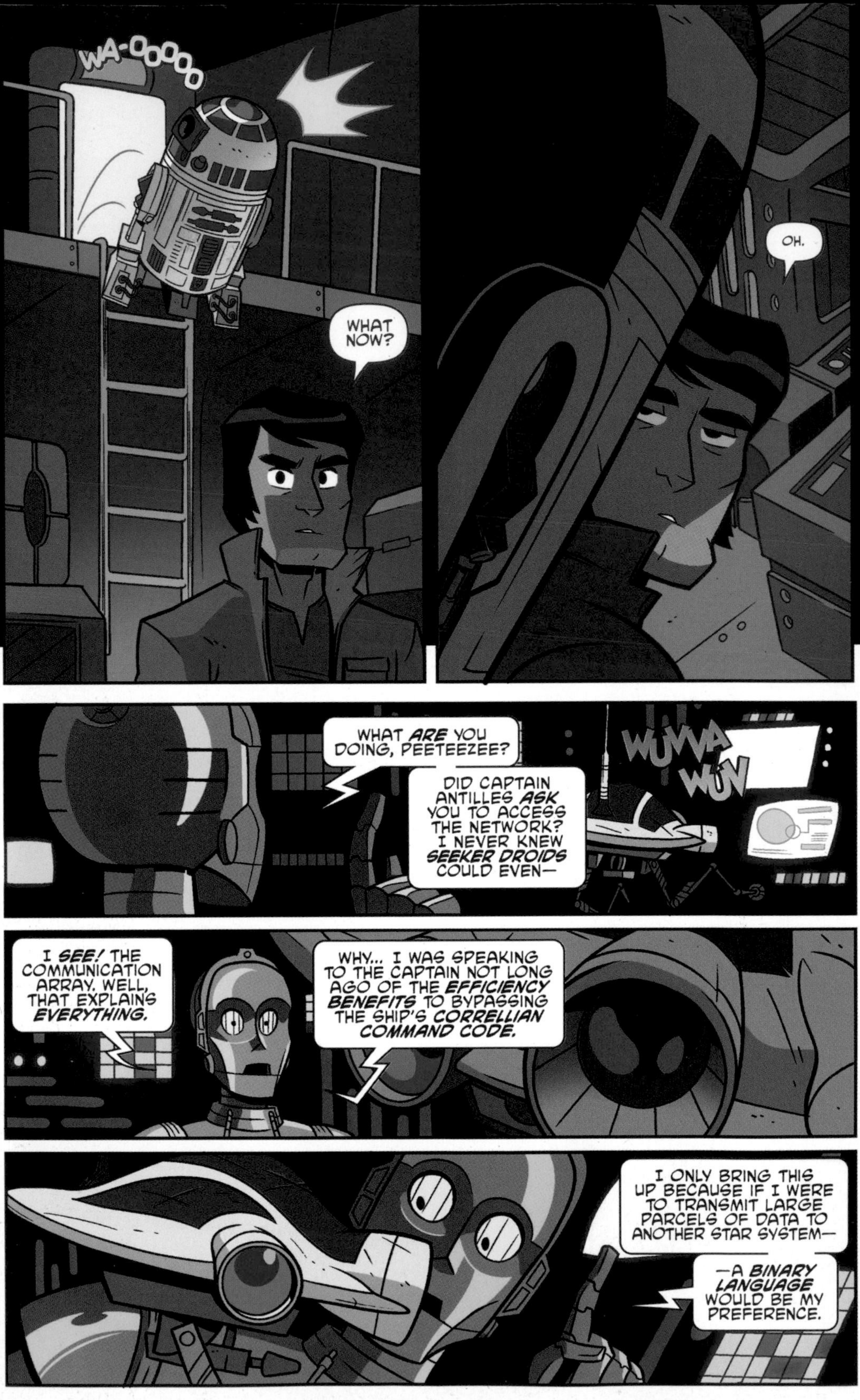
WA-OOOOO
WHAT NOW?
OH.
WHAT ARE YOU DOING, PEETEEZEE?
DID CAPTAIN ANTILLES ASK YOU TO ACCESS THE NETWORK? I NEVER KNEW SEEKER DROIDS COULD EVEN—
WUVVA WUV
I SEE! THE COMMUNICATION ARRAY. WELL, THAT EXPLAINS EVERYTHING.
WHY... I WAS SPEAKING TO THE CAPTAIN NOT LONG AGO OF THE EFFICIENCY BENEFITS TO BYPASSING THE SHIP'S CORRELLIAN COMMAND CODE.
I ONLY BRING THIS UP BECAUSE IF I WERE TO TRANSMIT LARGE PARCELS OF DATA TO ANOTHER STAR SYSTEM—
—A BINARY LANGUAGE WOULD BE MY PREFERENCE.

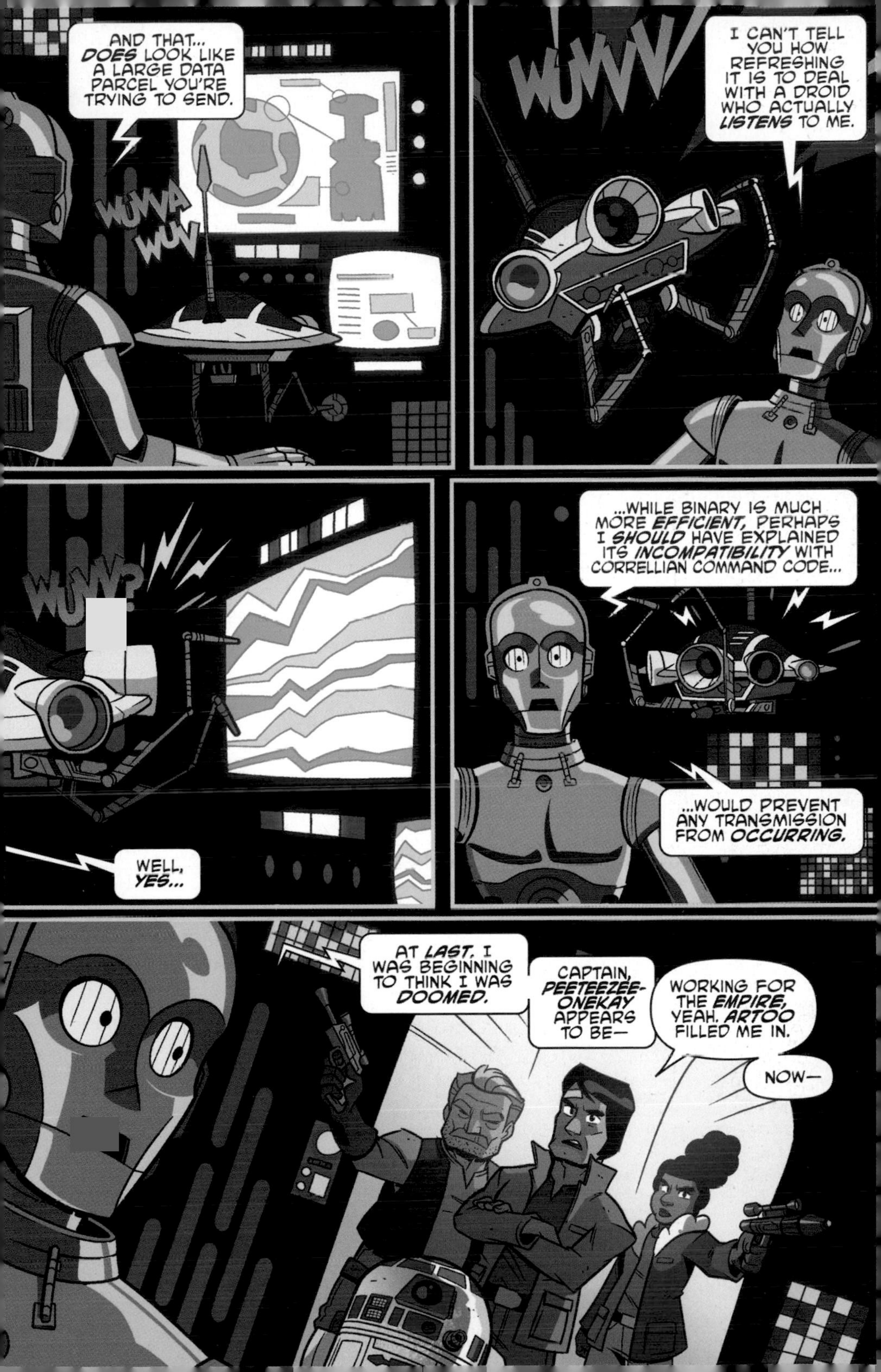
AND THAT... DOES LOOK LIKE A LARGE DATA PARCEL YOU'RE TRYING TO SEND.
WUVVA WUV
WUVVV
I CAN'T TELL YOU HOW REFRESHING IT IS TO DEAL WITH A DROID WHO ACTUALLY LISTENS TO ME.
WUVV?
WELL, YES...
...WHILE BINARY IS MUCH MORE EFFICIENT, PERHAPS I SHOULD HAVE EXPLAINED ITS INCOMPATIBILITY WITH CORRELLIAN COMMAND CODE...
...WOULD PREVENT ANY TRANSMISSION FROM OCCURRING.
AT LAST. I WAS BEGINNING TO THINK I WAS DOOMED.
CAPTAIN, PEETEEZEE-ONEKAY APPEARS TO BE—
WORKING FOR THE EMPIRE, YEAH. ARTOO FILLED ME IN.
NOW—

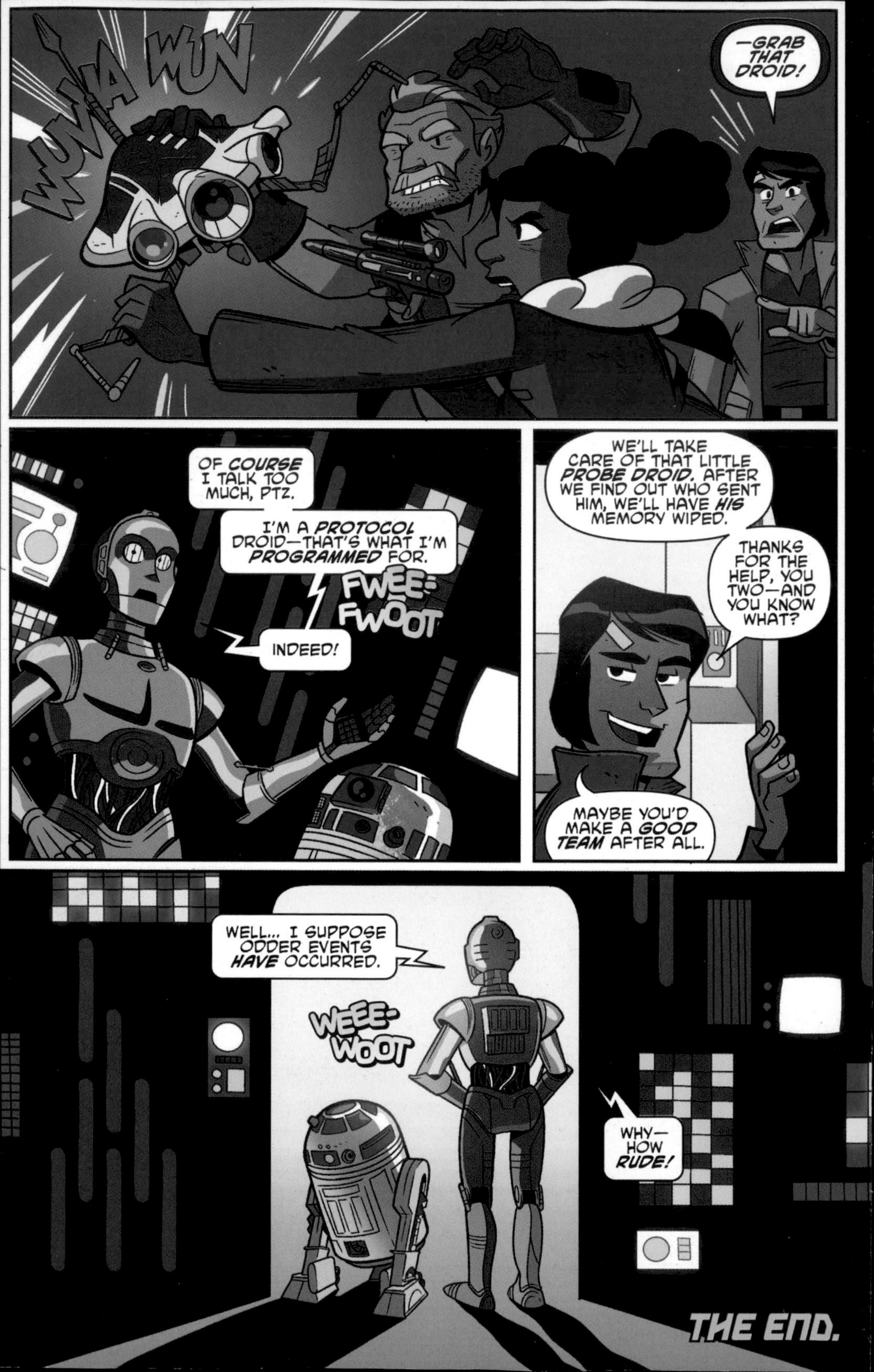
WUWA WUN
—GRAB THAT DROID!
OF COURSE I TALK TOO MUCH, PTZ.
I'M A PROTOCOL DROID—THAT'S WHAT I'M PROGRAMMED FOR.
FWEE-FWOOT
INDEED!
WE'LL TAKE CARE OF THAT LITTLE PROBE DROID. AFTER WE FIND OUT WHO SENT HIM, WE'LL HAVE HIS MEMORY WIPED.
THANKS FOR THE HELP, YOU TWO—AND YOU KNOW WHAT?
MAYBE YOU'D MAKE A GOOD TEAM AFTER ALL.
WELL... I SUPPOSE ODDER EVENTS HAVE OCCURRED.
WEEE-WOOT
WHY—HOW RUDE!
THE END.

STAR WARS™ ADVENTURES

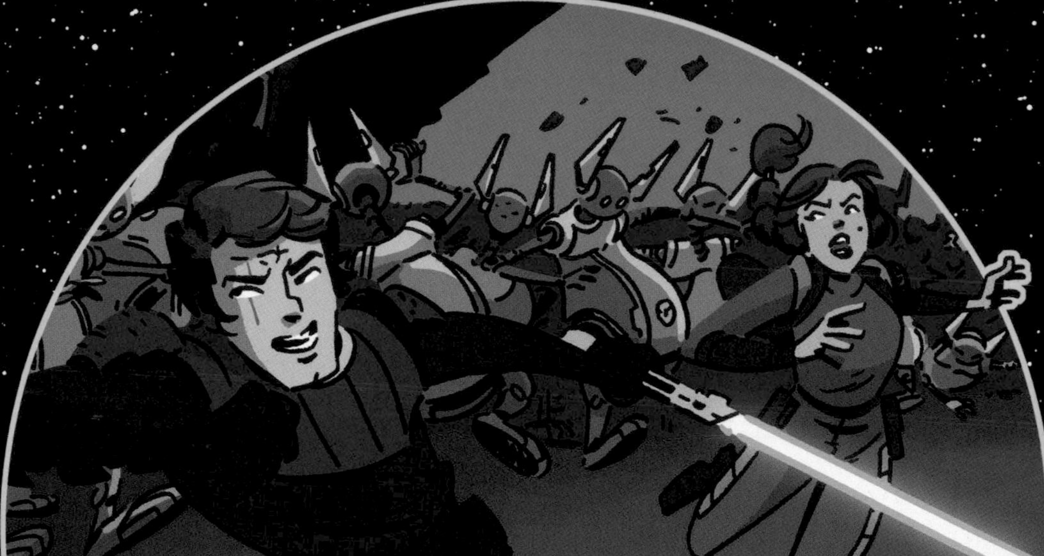

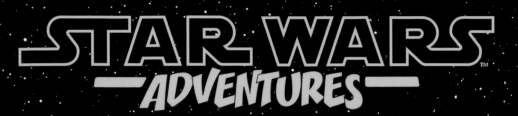

Intermission

WRITERS
ELSA CHARRETIER & PIERRICK COLINET
ARTIST
ELSA CHARRETIER
COLORIST
SARAH STERN

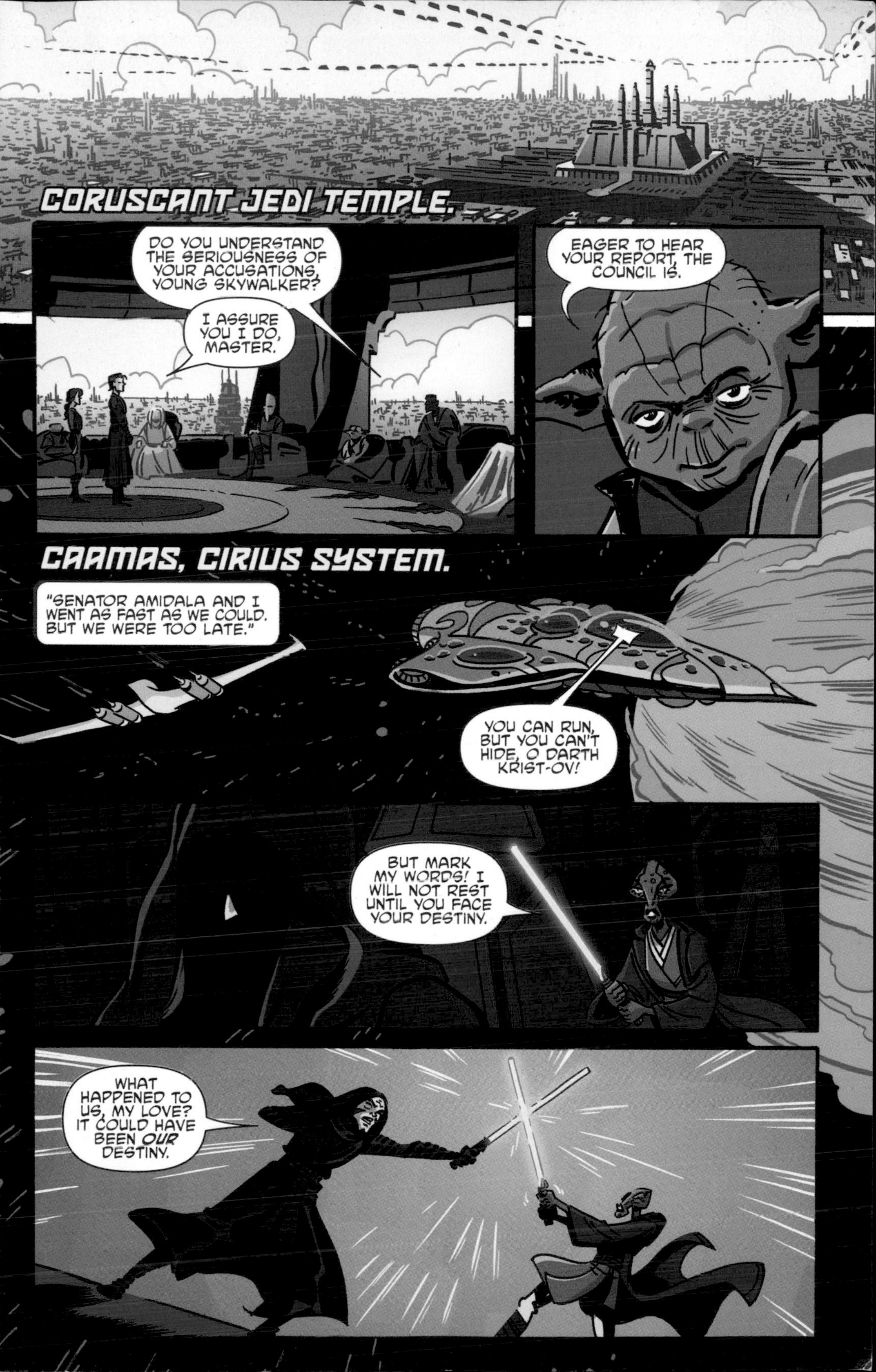
CORUSCANT JEDI TEMPLE.
DO YOU UNDERSTAND THE SERIOUSNESS OF YOUR ACCUSATIONS, YOUNG SKYWALKER?
I ASSURE YOU I DO, MASTER.
EAGER TO HEAR YOUR REPORT, THE COUNCIL IS.
CAAMAS, CIRIUS SYSTEM.
"SENATOR AMIDALA AND I WENT AS FAST AS WE COULD. BUT WE WERE TOO LATE."
YOU CAN RUN, BUT YOU CAN'T HIDE, O DARTH KRIST-OV!
BUT MARK MY WORDS! I WILL NOT REST UNTIL YOU FACE YOUR DESTINY.
WHAT HAPPENED TO US, MY LOVE? IT COULD HAVE BEEN *OUR* DESTINY.

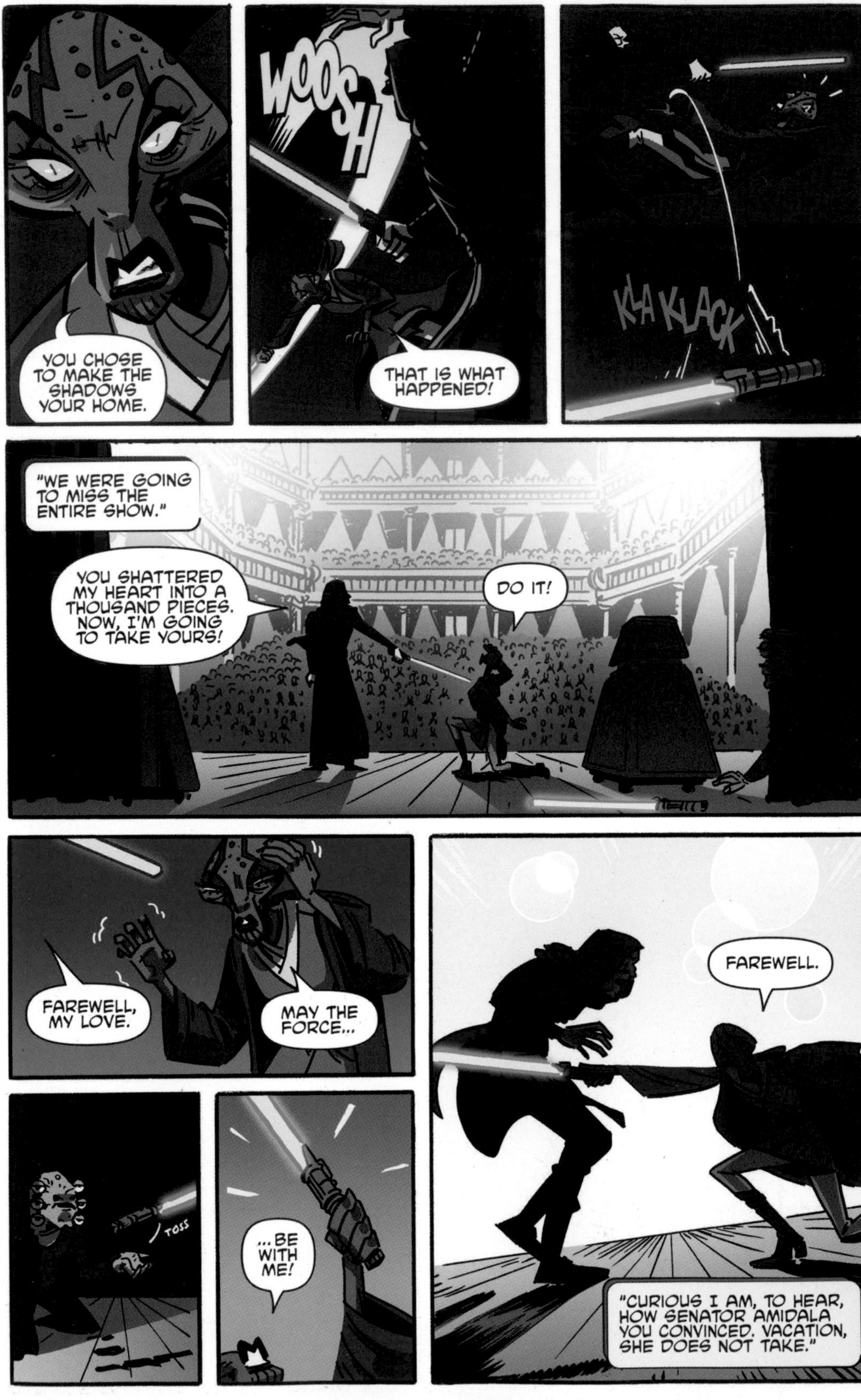

YOU CHOSE TO MAKE THE SHADOWS YOUR HOME.
WOOSH
THAT IS WHAT HAPPENED!
KLA KLACK
"WE WERE GOING TO MISS THE ENTIRE SHOW."
YOU SHATTERED MY HEART INTO A THOUSAND PIECES. NOW, I'M GOING TO TAKE YOURS!
DO IT!
FAREWELL, MY LOVE.
MAY THE FORCE...
FAREWELL.
TOSS
...BE WITH ME!
"CURIOUS I AM, TO HEAR, HOW SENATOR AMIDALA YOU CONVINCED. VACATION, SHE DOES NOT TAKE."

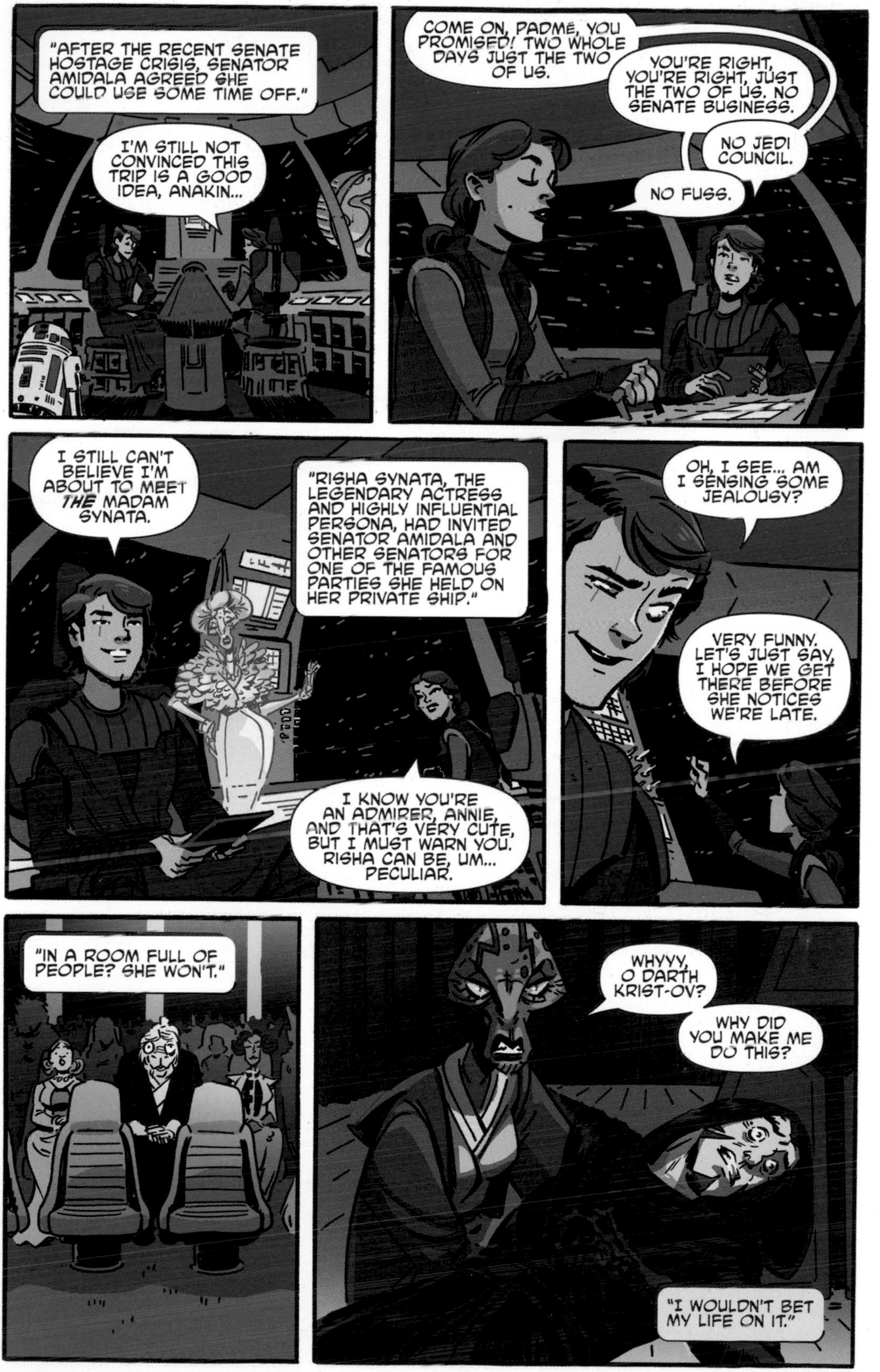
"AFTER THE RECENT SENATE HOSTAGE CRISIS, SENATOR AMIDALA AGREED SHE COULD USE SOME TIME OFF."
I'M STILL NOT CONVINCED THIS TRIP IS A GOOD IDEA, ANAKIN...
COME ON, PADME, YOU PROMISED! TWO WHOLE DAYS JUST THE TWO OF US.
YOU'RE RIGHT, YOU'RE RIGHT, JUST THE TWO OF US. NO SENATE BUSINESS.
NO JEDI COUNCIL.
NO FUSS.
I STILL CAN'T BELIEVE I'M ABOUT TO MEET *THE* MADAM SYNATA.
"RISHA SYNATA, THE LEGENDARY ACTRESS AND HIGHLY INFLUENTIAL PERSONA, HAD INVITED SENATOR AMIDALA AND OTHER SENATORS FOR ONE OF THE FAMOUS PARTIES SHE HELD ON HER PRIVATE SHIP."
I KNOW YOU'RE AN ADMIRER, ANNIE, AND THAT'S VERY CUTE, BUT I MUST WARN YOU. RISHA CAN BE, UM... PECULIAR.
OH, I SEE... AM I SENSING SOME JEALOUSY?
VERY FUNNY. LET'S JUST SAY, I HOPE WE GET THERE BEFORE SHE NOTICES WE'RE LATE.
"IN A ROOM FULL OF PEOPLE? SHE WON'T."
WHYYY, O DARTH KRIST-OV?
WHY DID YOU MAKE ME DO THIS?
"I WOULDN'T BET MY LIFE ON IT."

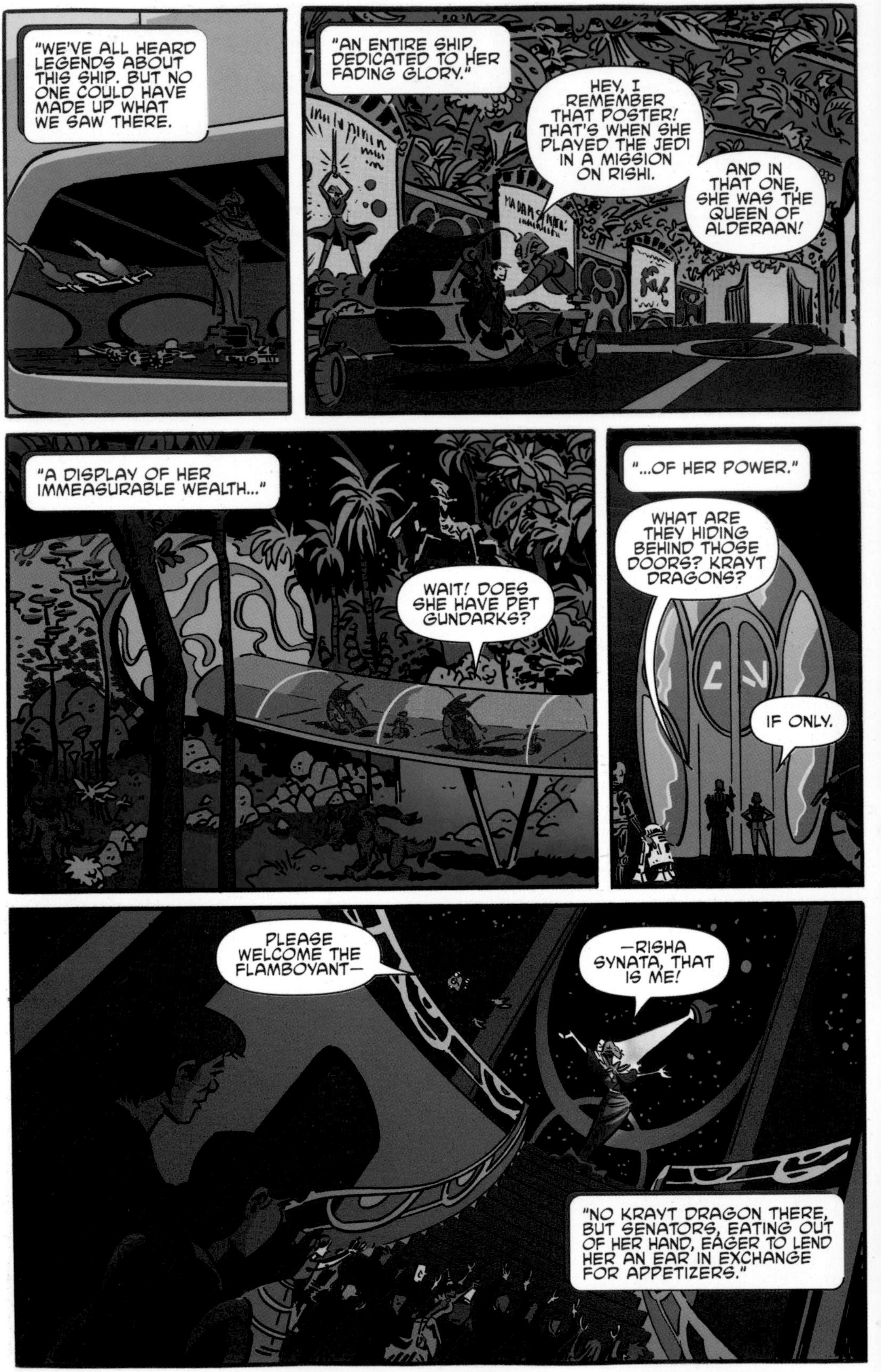
"WE'VE ALL HEARD LEGENDS ABOUT THIS SHIP. BUT NO ONE COULD HAVE MADE UP WHAT WE SAW THERE.
"AN ENTIRE SHIP, DEDICATED TO HER FADING GLORY."
HEY, I REMEMBER THAT POSTER! THAT'S WHEN SHE PLAYED THE JEDI IN A MISSION ON RISHI.
AND IN THAT ONE, SHE WAS THE QUEEN OF ALDERAAN!
"A DISPLAY OF HER IMMEASURABLE WEALTH..."
WAIT! DOES SHE HAVE PET GUNDARKS?
"...OF HER POWER."
WHAT ARE THEY HIDING BEHIND THOSE DOORS? KRAYT DRAGONS?
IF ONLY.
PLEASE WELCOME THE FLAMBOYANT—
—RISHA SYNATA, THAT IS ME!
"NO KRAYT DRAGON THERE, BUT SENATORS, EATING OUT OF HER HAND, EAGER TO LEND HER AN EAR IN EXCHANGE FOR APPETIZERS."

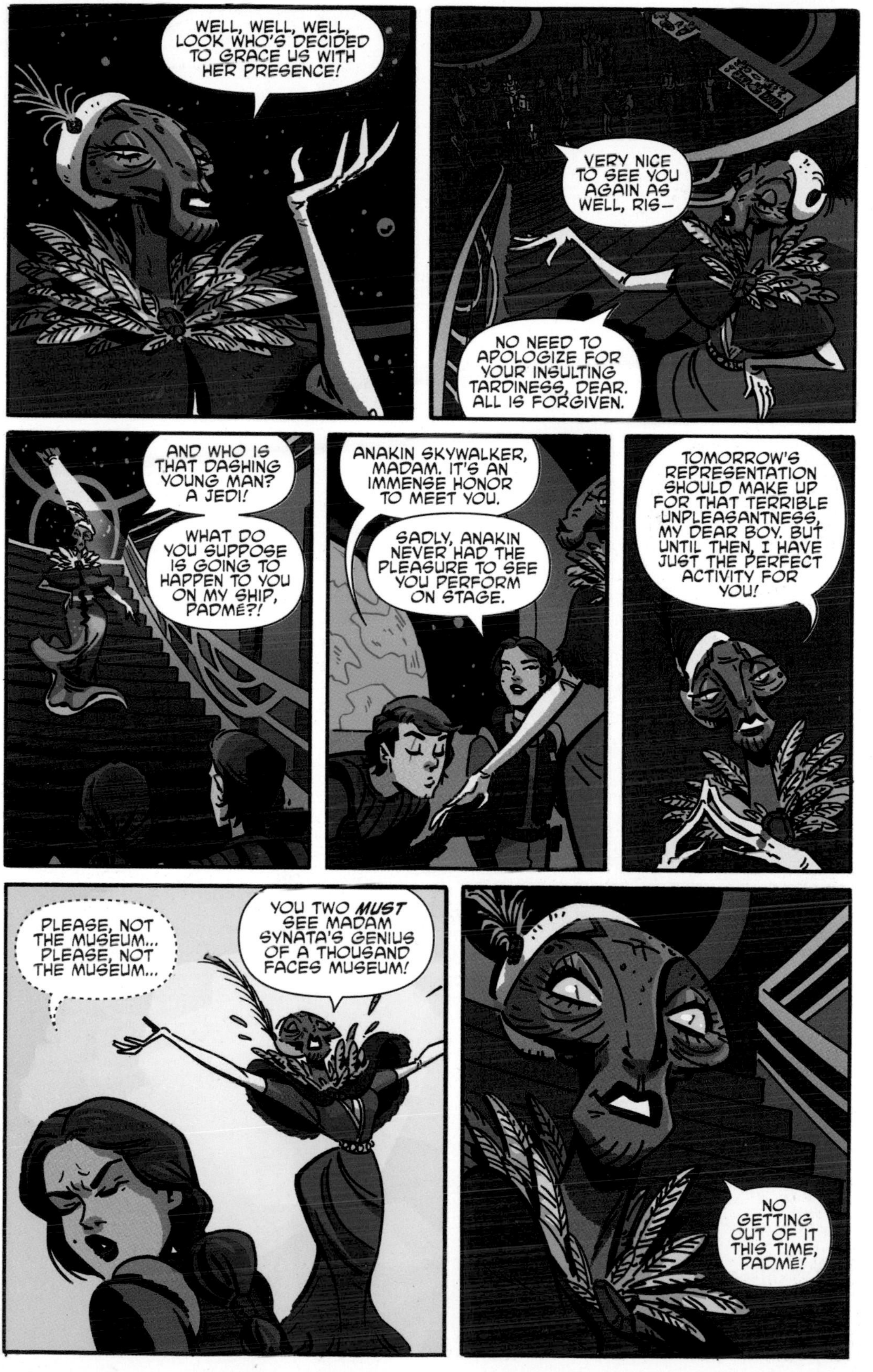
WELL, WELL, WELL, LOOK WHO'S DECIDED TO GRACE US WITH HER PRESENCE!
VERY NICE TO SEE YOU AGAIN AS WELL, RIS—
NO NEED TO APOLOGIZE FOR YOUR INSULTING TARDINESS, DEAR. ALL IS FORGIVEN.
AND WHO IS THAT DASHING YOUNG MAN? A JEDI!
WHAT DO YOU SUPPOSE IS GOING TO HAPPEN TO YOU ON MY SHIP, PADMÉ?!
ANAKIN SKYWALKER, MADAM. IT'S AN IMMENSE HONOR TO MEET YOU.
SADLY, ANAKIN NEVER HAD THE PLEASURE TO SEE YOU PERFORM ON STAGE.
TOMORROW'S REPRESENTATION SHOULD MAKE UP FOR THAT TERRIBLE UNPLEASANTNESS, MY DEAR BOY. BUT UNTIL THEN, I HAVE JUST THE PERFECT ACTIVITY FOR YOU!
YOU TWO *MUST* SEE MADAM SYNATA'S GENIUS OF A THOUSAND FACES MUSEUM!
PLEASE, NOT THE MUSEUM... PLEASE, NOT THE MUSEUM...
NO GETTING OUT OF IT THIS TIME, PADMÉ!

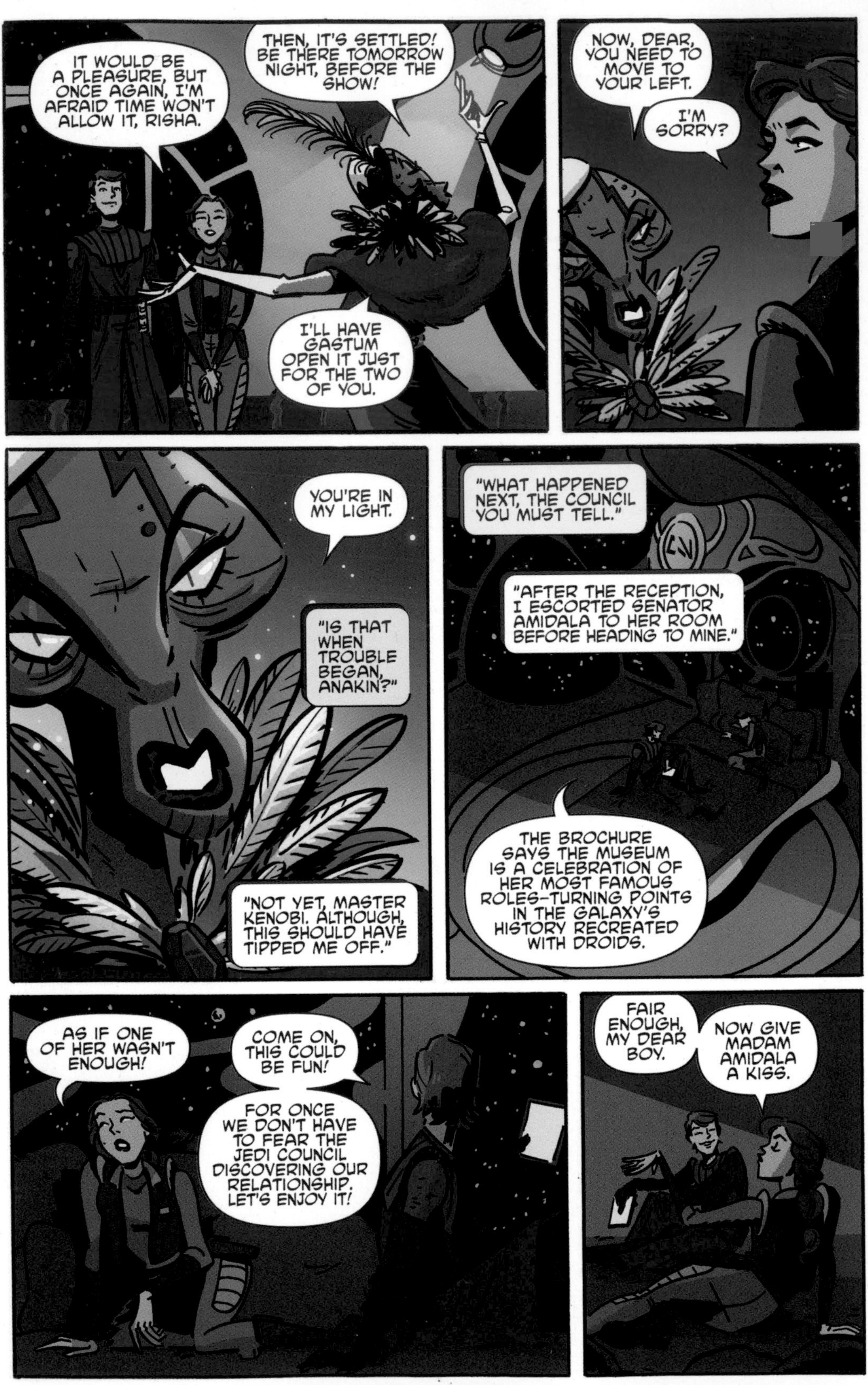
IT WOULD BE A PLEASURE, BUT ONCE AGAIN, I'M AFRAID TIME WON'T ALLOW IT, RISHA.
THEN, IT'S SETTLED! BE THERE TOMORROW NIGHT, BEFORE THE SHOW!
I'LL HAVE GASTUM OPEN IT JUST FOR THE TWO OF YOU.
NOW, DEAR, YOU NEED TO MOVE TO YOUR LEFT.
I'M SORRY?
YOU'RE IN MY LIGHT.
"IS THAT WHEN TROUBLE BEGAN, ANAKIN?"
"NOT YET, MASTER KENOBI. ALTHOUGH, THIS SHOULD HAVE TIPPED ME OFF."
"WHAT HAPPENED NEXT, THE COUNCIL YOU MUST TELL."
"AFTER THE RECEPTION, I ESCORTED SENATOR AMIDALA TO HER ROOM BEFORE HEADING TO MINE."
THE BROCHURE SAYS THE MUSEUM IS A CELEBRATION OF HER MOST FAMOUS ROLES–TURNING POINTS IN THE GALAXY'S HISTORY RECREATED WITH DROIDS.
AS IF ONE OF HER WASN'T ENOUGH!
COME ON, THIS COULD BE FUN!
FOR ONCE WE DON'T HAVE TO FEAR THE JEDI COUNCIL DISCOVERING OUR RELATIONSHIP. LET'S ENJOY IT!
FAIR ENOUGH, MY DEAR BOY.
NOW GIVE MADAM AMIDALA A KISS.

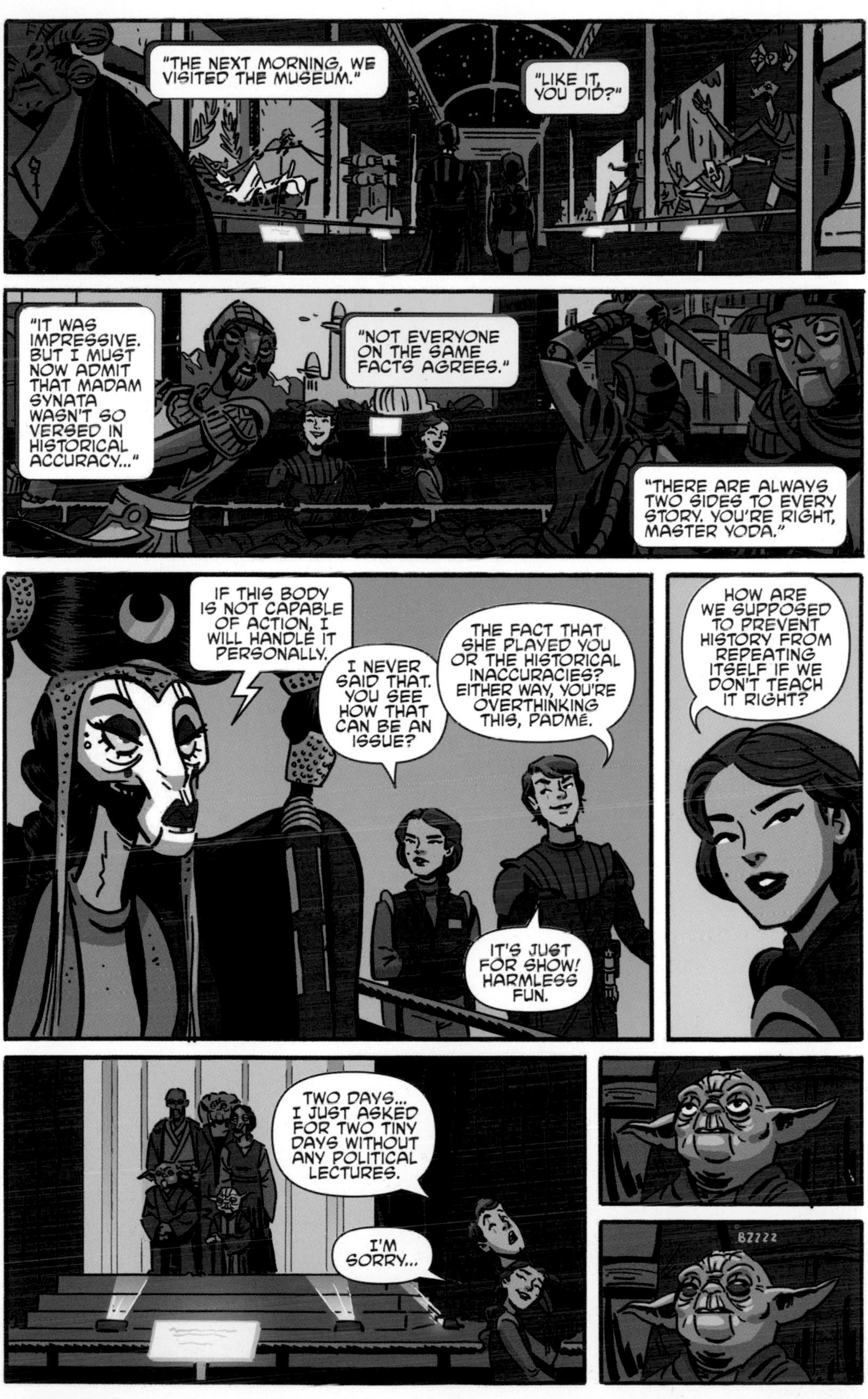
"THE NEXT MORNING, WE VISITED THE MUSEUM."
"LIKE IT, YOU DID?"
"IT WAS IMPRESSIVE. BUT I MUST NOW ADMIT THAT MADAM SYNATA WASN'T SO VERSED IN HISTORICAL ACCURACY..."
"NOT EVERYONE ON THE SAME FACTS AGREES."
"THERE ARE ALWAYS TWO SIDES TO EVERY STORY. YOU'RE RIGHT, MASTER YODA."
IF THIS BODY IS NOT CAPABLE OF ACTION, I WILL HANDLE IT PERSONALLY.
I NEVER SAID THAT. YOU SEE HOW THAT CAN BE AN ISSUE?
THE FACT THAT SHE PLAYED YOU OR THE HISTORICAL INACCURACIES? EITHER WAY, YOU'RE OVERTHINKING THIS, PADMÉ.
IT'S JUST FOR SHOW! HARMLESS FUN.
HOW ARE WE SUPPOSED TO PREVENT HISTORY FROM REPEATING ITSELF IF WE DON'T TEACH IT RIGHT?
TWO DAYS... I JUST ASKED FOR TWO TINY DAYS WITHOUT ANY POLITICAL LECTURES.
I'M SORRY...
BZZZZ

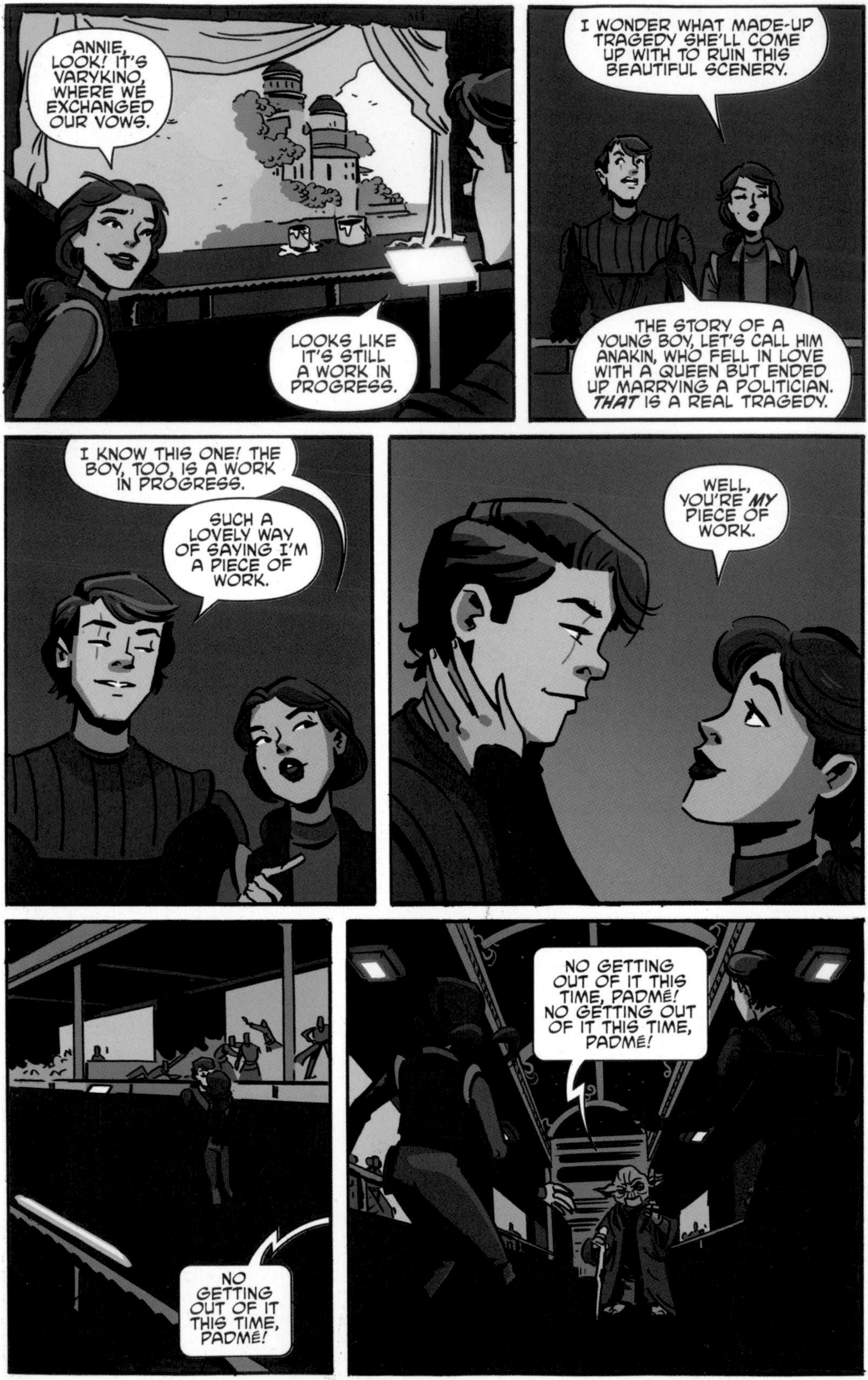
ANNIE, LOOK! IT'S VARYKINO, WHERE WE EXCHANGED OUR VOWS.
LOOKS LIKE IT'S STILL A WORK IN PROGRESS.
I WONDER WHAT MADE-UP TRAGEDY SHE'LL COME UP WITH TO RUIN THIS BEAUTIFUL SCENERY.
THE STORY OF A YOUNG BOY, LET'S CALL HIM ANAKIN, WHO FELL IN LOVE WITH A QUEEN BUT ENDED UP MARRYING A POLITICIAN. *THAT* IS A REAL TRAGEDY.
I KNOW THIS ONE! THE BOY, TOO, IS A WORK IN PROGRESS.
SUCH A LOVELY WAY OF SAYING I'M A PIECE OF WORK.
WELL, YOU'RE *MY* PIECE OF WORK.
NO GETTING OUT OF IT THIS TIME, PADMÉ!
NO GETTING OUT OF IT THIS TIME, PADMÉ! NO GETTING OUT OF IT THIS TIME, PADMÉ!

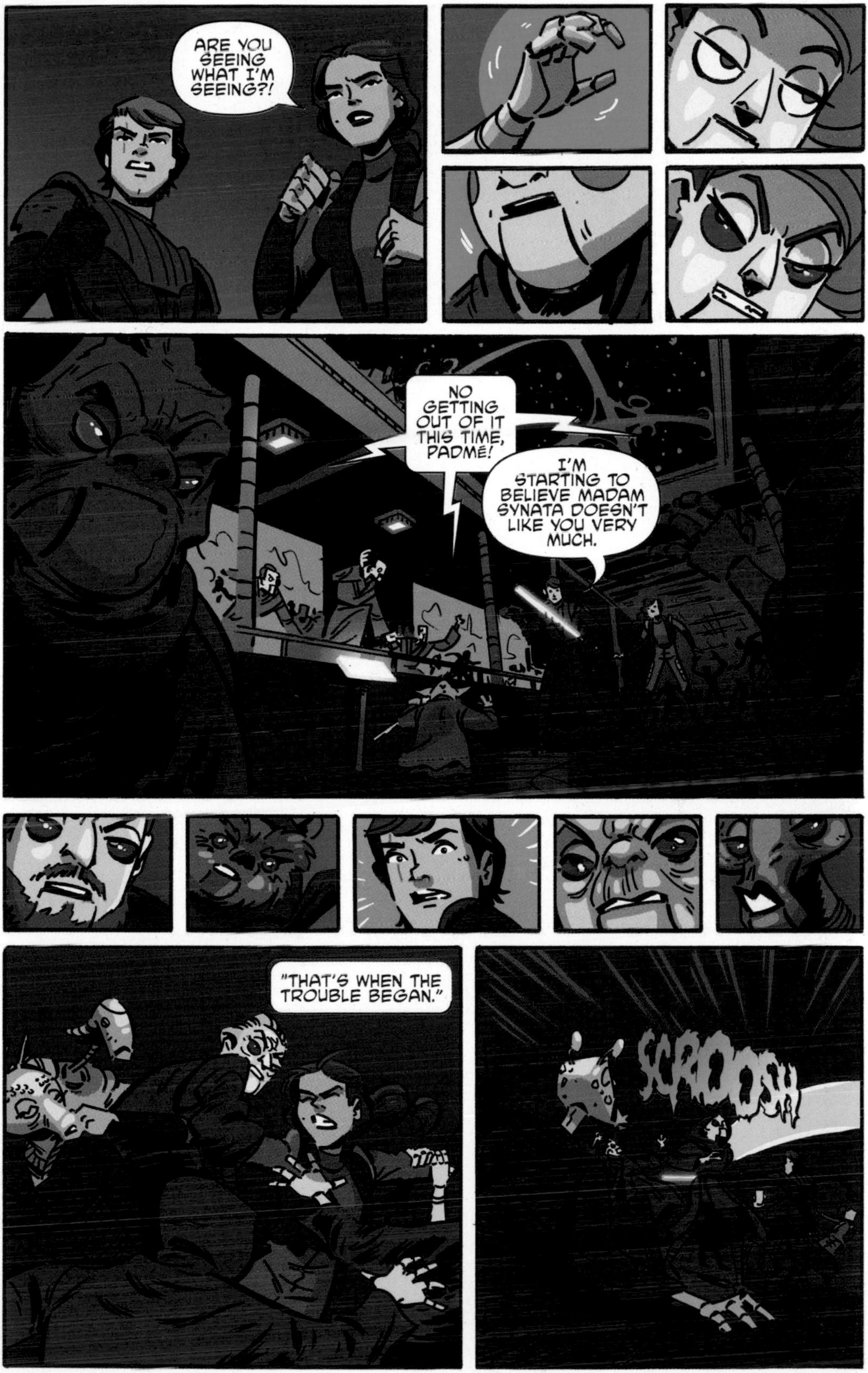

ARE YOU SEEING WHAT I'M SEEING?!
NO GETTING OUT OF IT THIS TIME, PADMÉ!
I'M STARTING TO BELIEVE MADAM SYNATA DOESN'T LIKE YOU VERY MUCH.
"THAT'S WHEN THE TROUBLE BEGAN."
SCROOSH

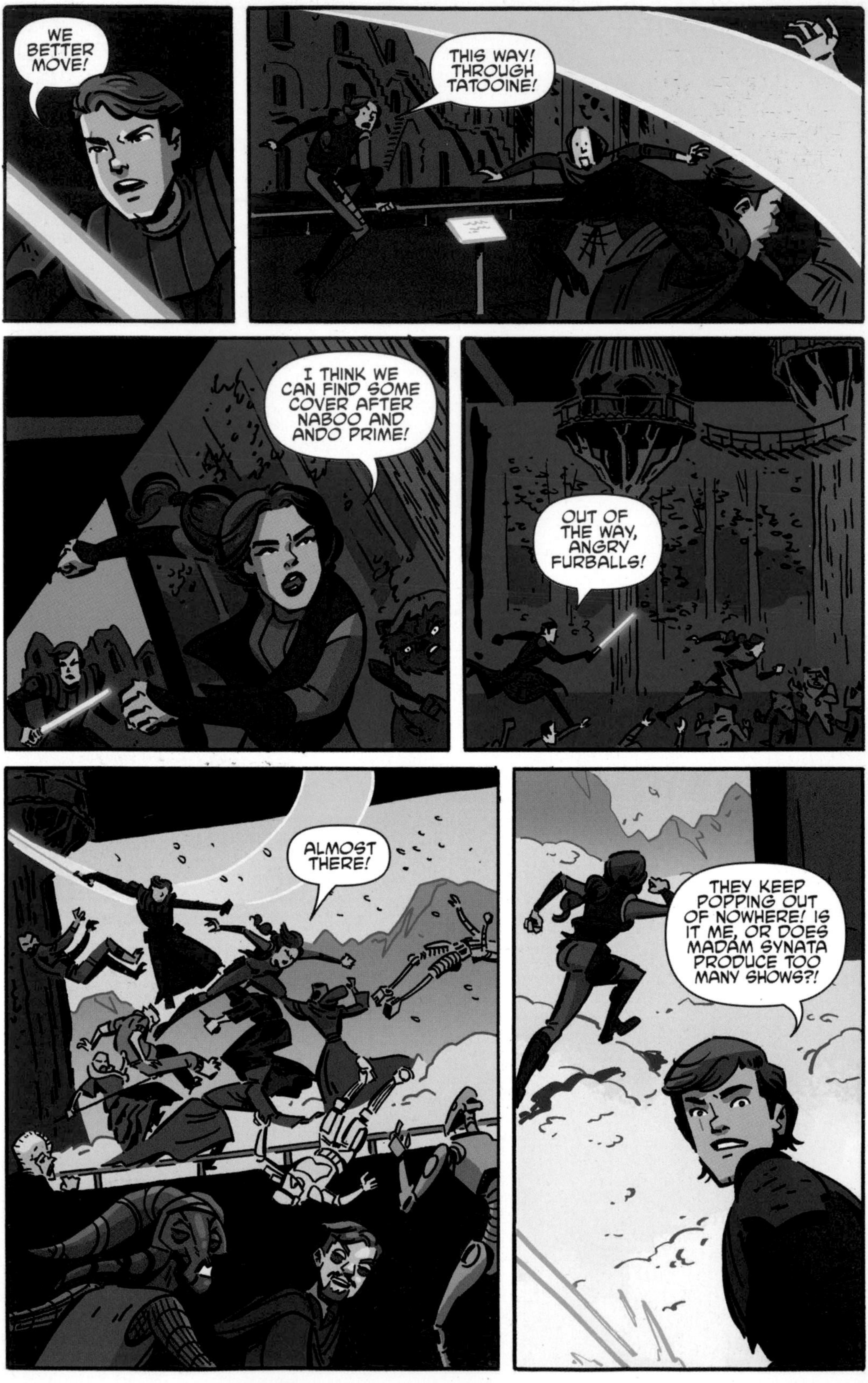
WE BETTER MOVE!
THIS WAY! THROUGH TATOOINE!
I THINK WE CAN FIND SOME COVER AFTER NABOO AND ANDO PRIME!
OUT OF THE WAY, ANGRY FURBALLS!
ALMOST THERE!
THEY KEEP POPPING OUT OF NOWHERE! IS IT ME, OR DOES MADAM SYNATA PRODUCE TOO MANY SHOWS?!

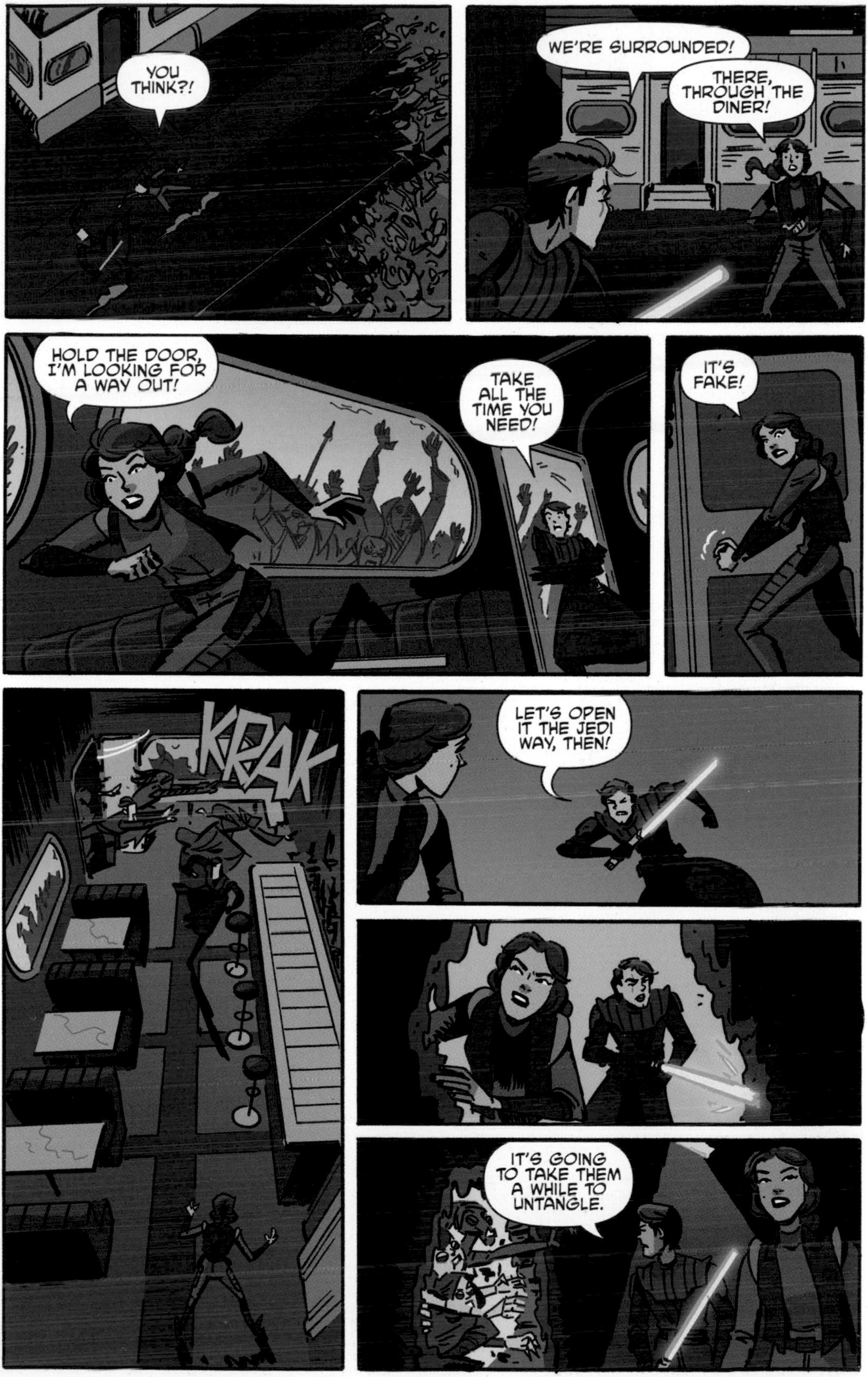
YOU THINK?!
WE'RE SURROUNDED!
THERE, THROUGH THE DINER!
HOLD THE DOOR, I'M LOOKING FOR A WAY OUT!
TAKE ALL THE TIME YOU NEED!
IT'S FAKE!
KRAK
LET'S OPEN IT THE JEDI WAY, THEN!
IT'S GOING TO TAKE THEM A WHILE TO UNTANGLE.

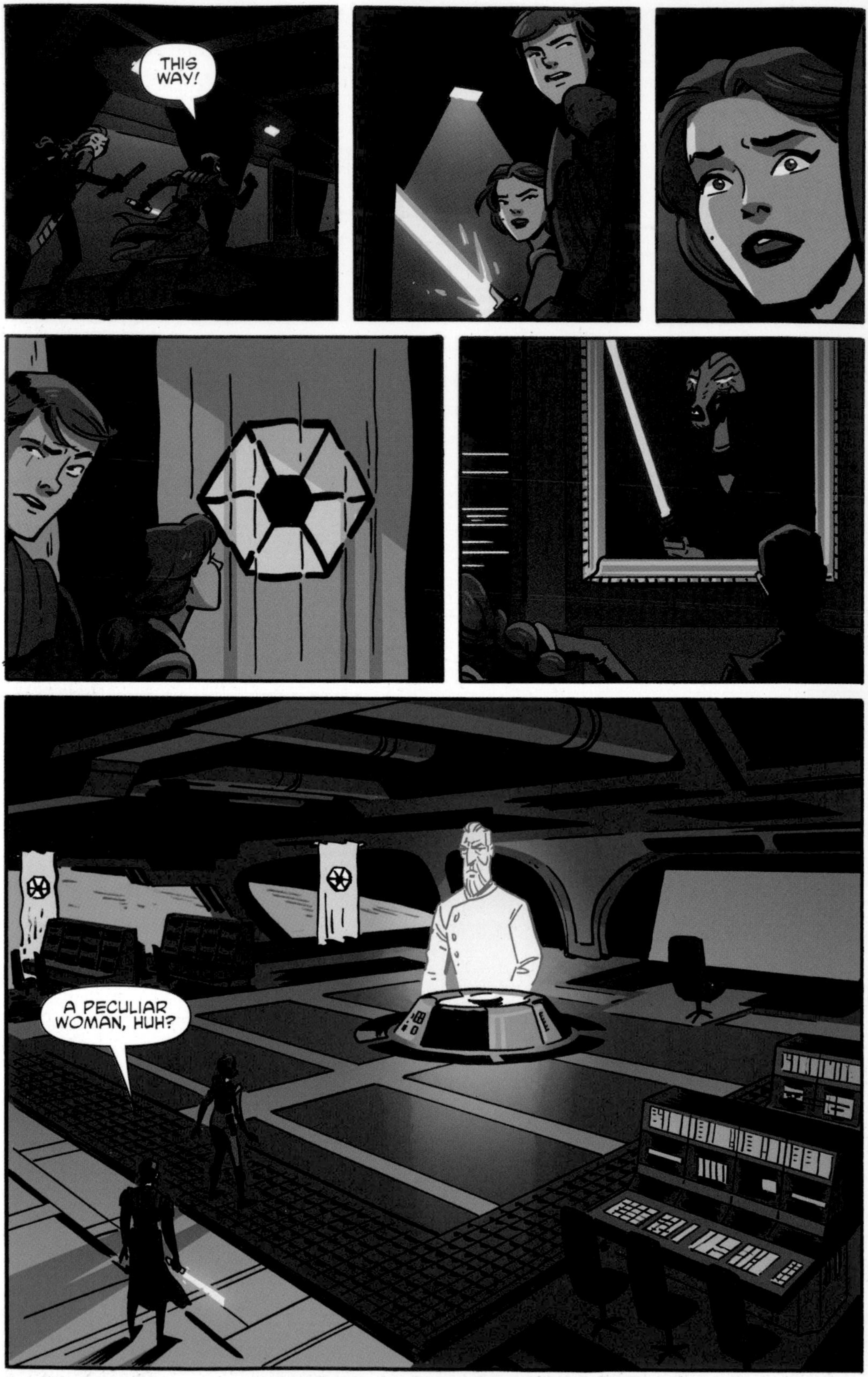
THIS WAY!
A PECULIAR WOMAN, HUH?

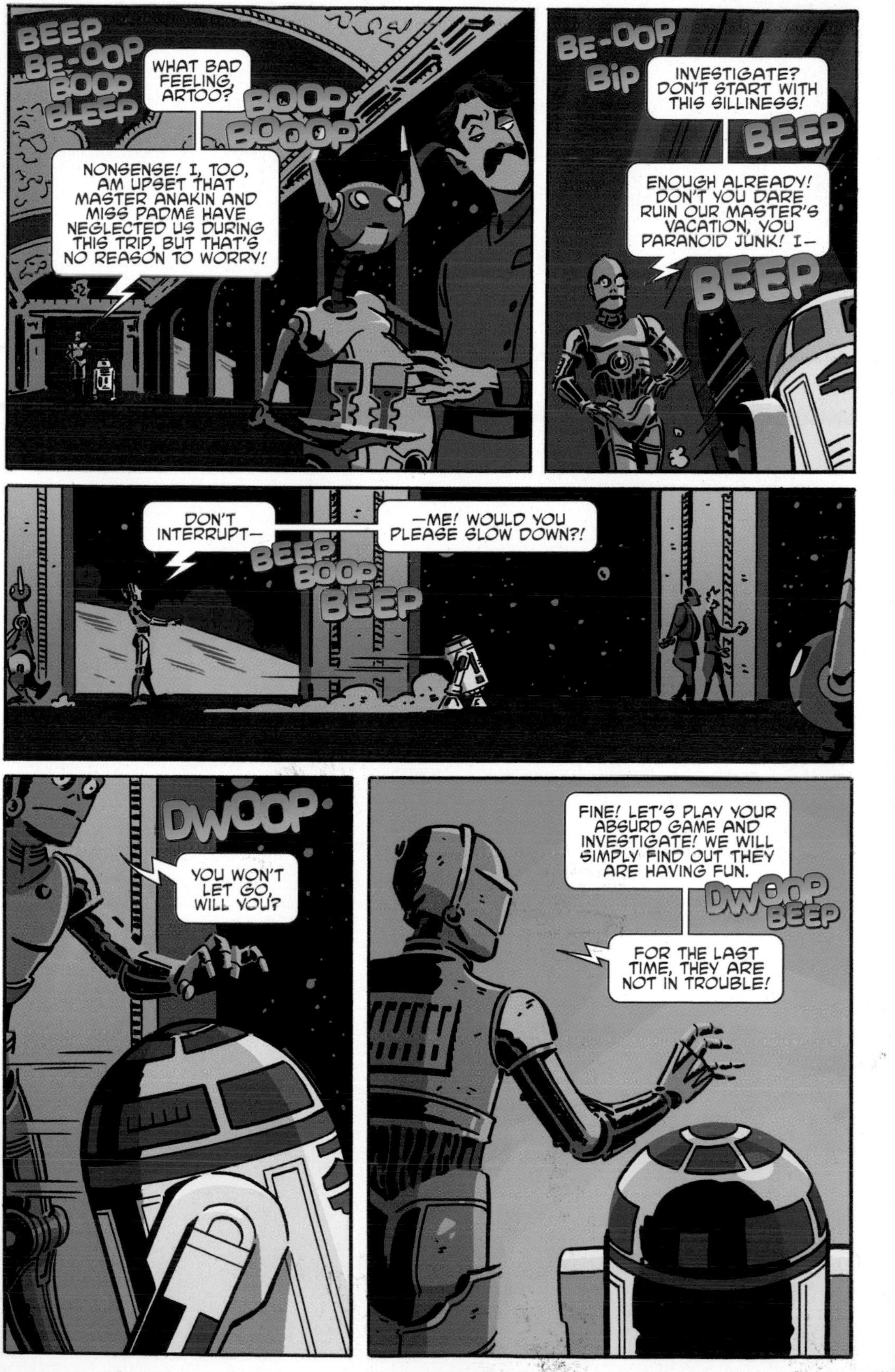
BEEP BE-OOP BOOP BLEEP
WHAT BAD FEELING, ARTOO?
BOOP BOOOP
NONSENSE! I, TOO, AM UPSET THAT MASTER ANAKIN AND MISS PADMÉ HAVE NEGLECTED US DURING THIS TRIP, BUT THAT'S NO REASON TO WORRY!
BE-OOP BIP
INVESTIGATE? DON'T START WITH THIS SILLINESS!
BEEP
ENOUGH ALREADY! DON'T YOU DARE RUIN OUR MASTER'S VACATION, YOU PARANOID JUNK! I—
BEEP
DON'T INTERRUPT—
—ME! WOULD YOU PLEASE SLOW DOWN?!
BEEP BOOP BEEP
DWOOP
YOU WON'T LET GO, WILL YOU?
FINE! LET'S PLAY YOUR ABSURD GAME AND INVESTIGATE! WE WILL SIMPLY FIND OUT THEY ARE HAVING FUN.
DWOOP BEEP
FOR THE LAST TIME, THEY ARE NOT IN TROUBLE!

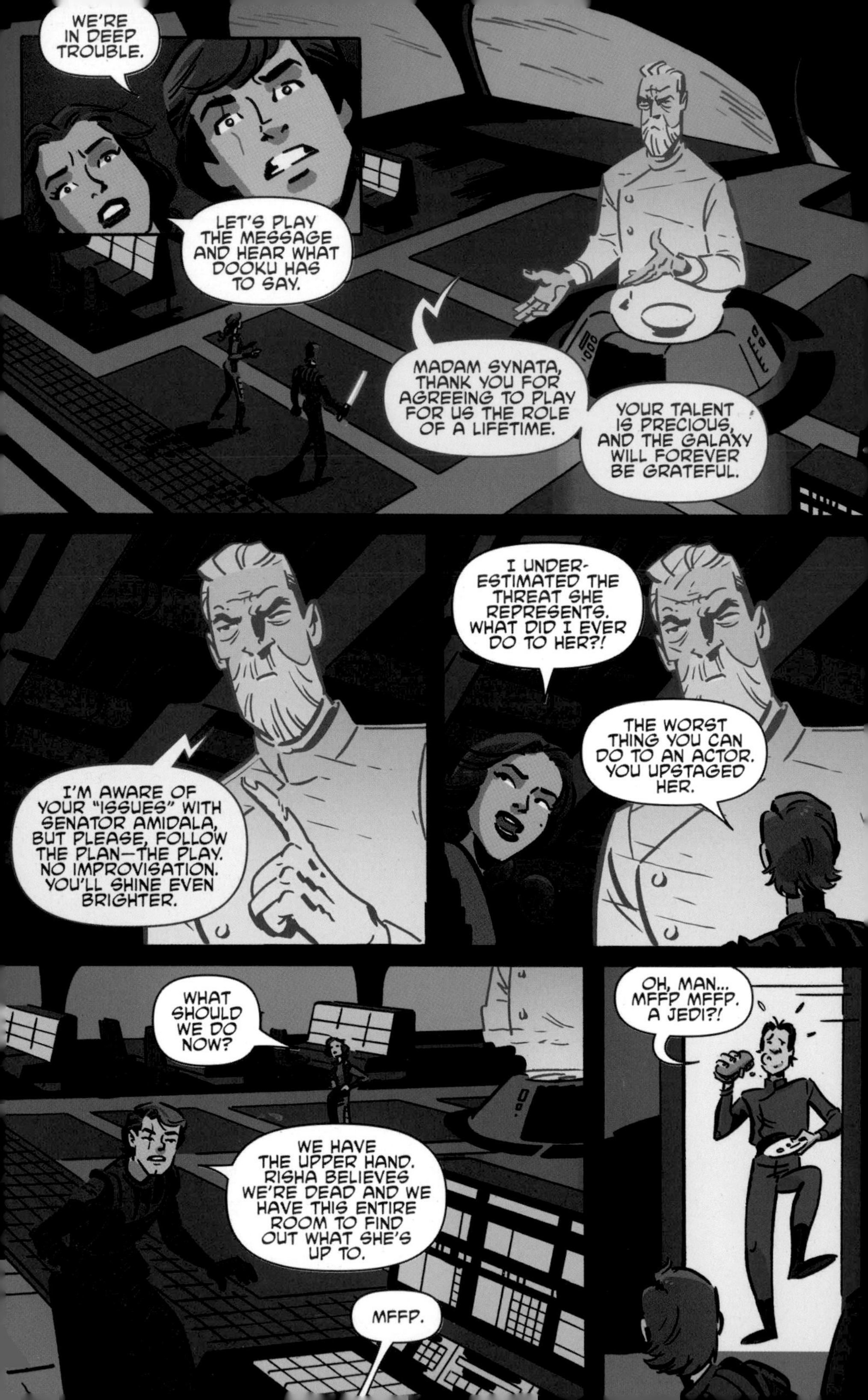
WE'RE IN DEEP TROUBLE.
LET'S PLAY THE MESSAGE AND HEAR WHAT DOOKU HAS TO SAY.
MADAM SYNATA, THANK YOU FOR AGREEING TO PLAY FOR US THE ROLE OF A LIFETIME.
YOUR TALENT IS PRECIOUS, AND THE GALAXY WILL FOREVER BE GRATEFUL.
I'M AWARE OF YOUR "ISSUES" WITH SENATOR AMIDALA, BUT PLEASE, FOLLOW THE PLAN—THE PLAY. NO IMPROVISATION. YOU'LL SHINE EVEN BRIGHTER.
I UNDER-ESTIMATED THE THREAT SHE REPRESENTS. WHAT DID I EVER DO TO HER?!
THE WORST THING YOU CAN DO TO AN ACTOR. YOU UPSTAGED HER.
WHAT SHOULD WE DO NOW?
WE HAVE THE UPPER HAND. RISHA BELIEVES WE'RE DEAD AND WE HAVE THIS ENTIRE ROOM TO FIND OUT WHAT SHE'S UP TO.
MFFP.
OH, MAN... MFFP MFFP. A JEDI?!

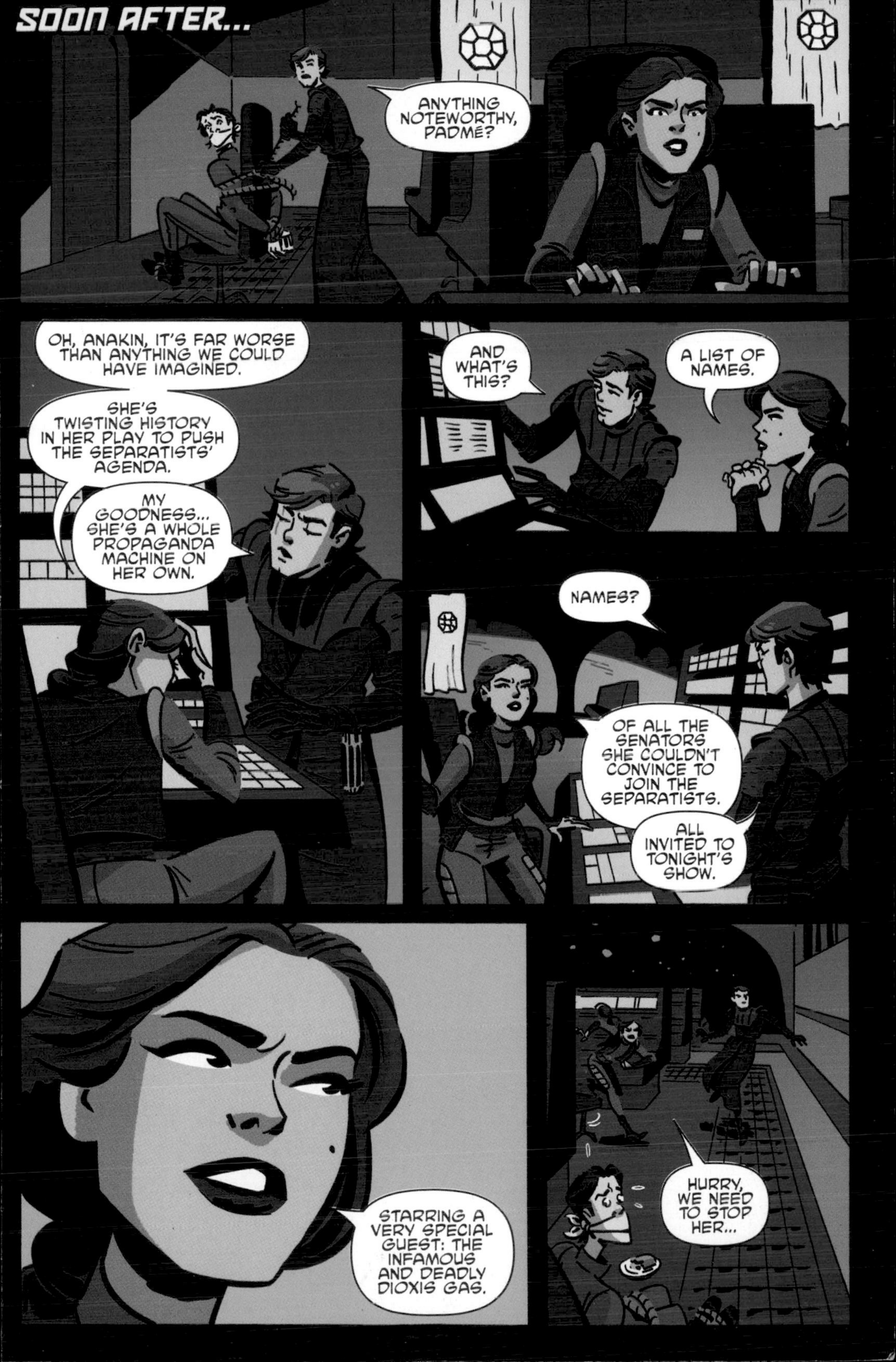
SOON AFTER...
ANYTHING NOTEWORTHY, PADMÉ?
OH, ANAKIN, IT'S FAR WORSE THAN ANYTHING WE COULD HAVE IMAGINED.
SHE'S TWISTING HISTORY IN HER PLAY TO PUSH THE SEPARATISTS' AGENDA.
MY GOODNESS... SHE'S A WHOLE PROPAGANDA MACHINE ON HER OWN.
AND WHAT'S THIS?
A LIST OF NAMES.
NAMES?
OF ALL THE SENATORS SHE COULDN'T CONVINCE TO JOIN THE SEPARATISTS.
ALL INVITED TO TONIGHT'S SHOW.
STARRING A VERY SPECIAL GUEST: THE INFAMOUS AND DEADLY DIOXIS GAS.
HURRY, WE NEED TO STOP HER...

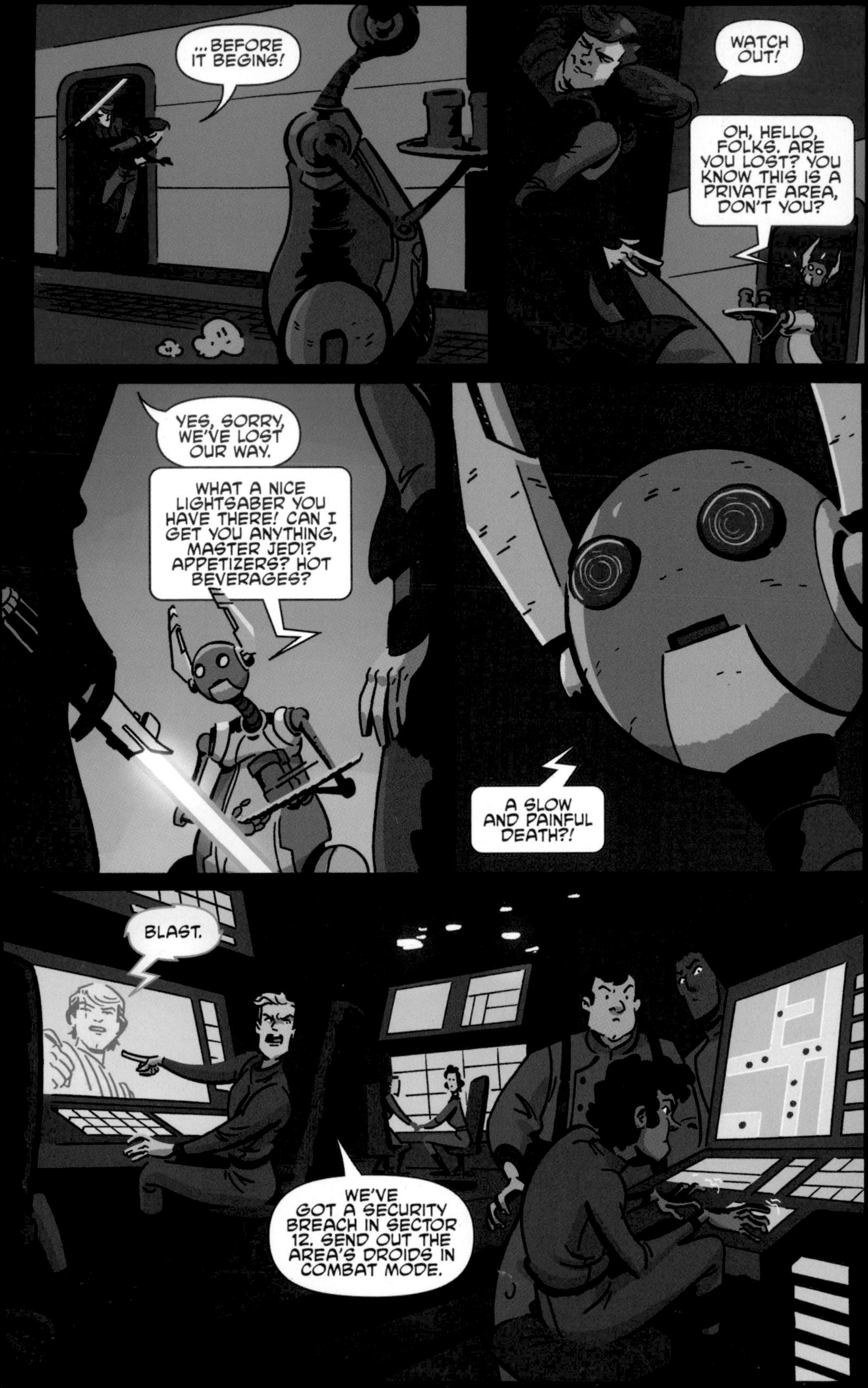
...BEFORE IT BEGINS!
WATCH OUT!
OH, HELLO, FOLKS. ARE YOU LOST? YOU KNOW THIS IS A PRIVATE AREA, DON'T YOU?
YES, SORRY, WE'VE LOST OUR WAY.
WHAT A NICE LIGHTSABER YOU HAVE THERE! CAN I GET YOU ANYTHING, MASTER JEDI? APPETIZERS? HOT BEVERAGES?
A SLOW AND PAINFUL DEATH?!
BLAST.
WE'VE GOT A SECURITY BREACH IN SECTOR 12. SEND OUT THE AREA'S DROIDS IN COMBAT MODE.

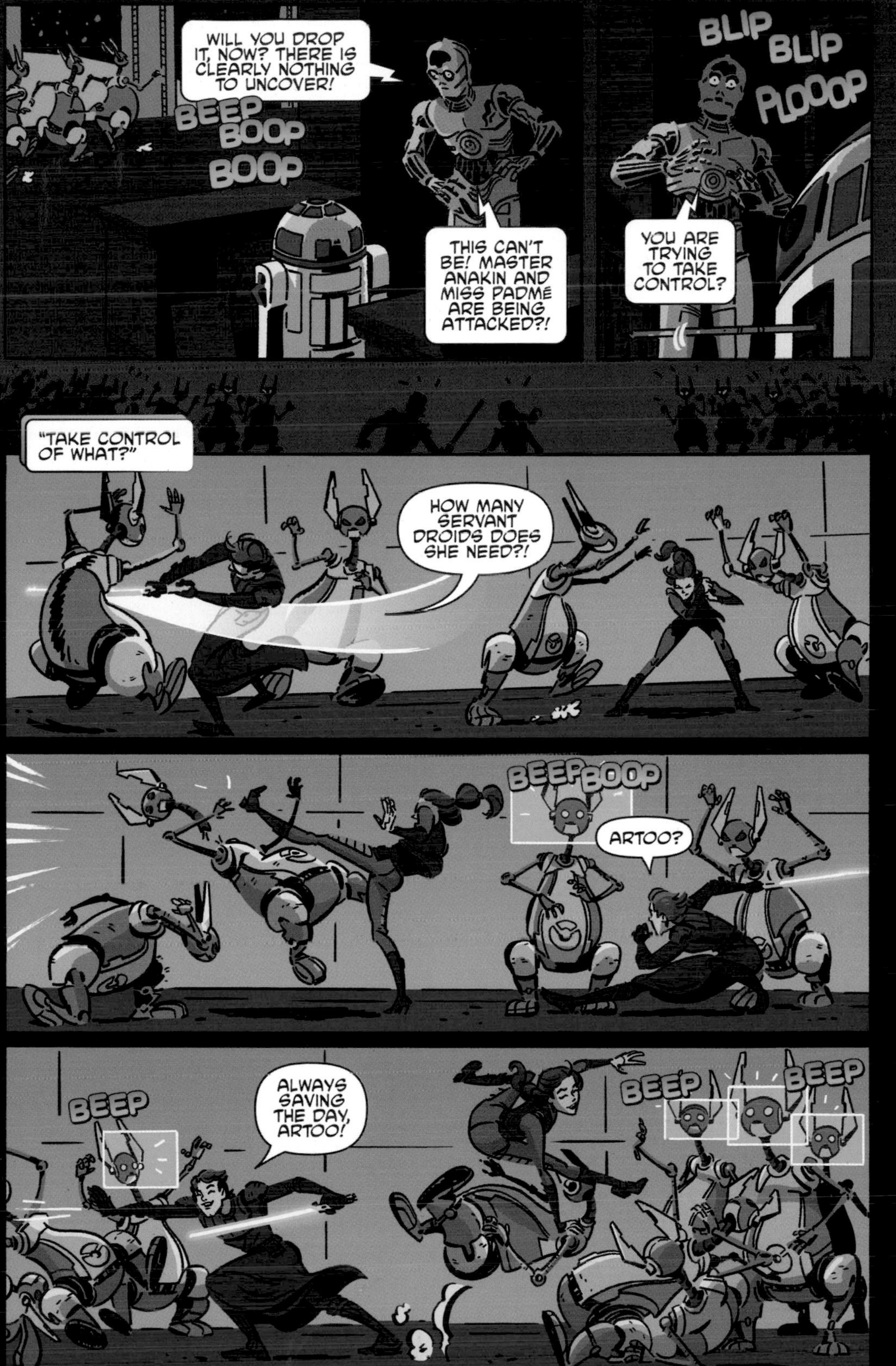
WILL YOU DROP IT, NOW? THERE IS CLEARLY NOTHING TO UNCOVER!
BEEP
BOOP
BOOP
THIS CAN'T BE! MASTER ANAKIN AND MISS PADMÉ ARE BEING ATTACKED?!
BLIP
BLIP
PLOOOP
YOU ARE TRYING TO TAKE CONTROL?
"TAKE CONTROL OF WHAT?"
HOW MANY SERVANT DROIDS DOES SHE NEED?!
BEEP BOOP
ARTOO?
BEEP
ALWAYS SAVING THE DAY, ARTOO!
BEEP
BEEP

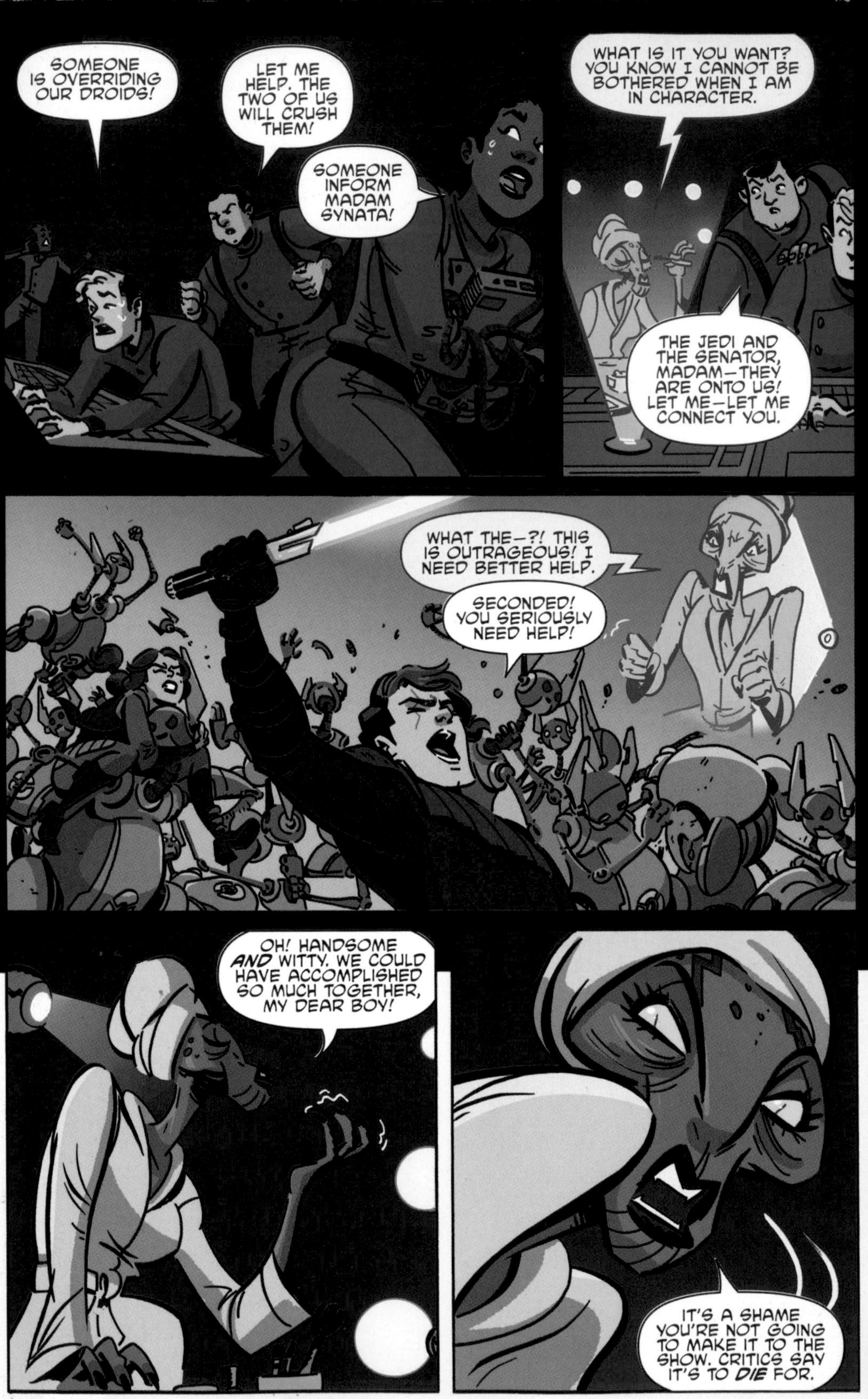

SOMEONE IS OVERRIDING OUR DROIDS!
LET ME HELP. THE TWO OF US WILL CRUSH THEM!
SOMEONE INFORM MADAM SYNATA!
WHAT IS IT YOU WANT? YOU KNOW I CANNOT BE BOTHERED WHEN I AM IN CHARACTER.
THE JEDI AND THE SENATOR, MADAM—THEY ARE ONTO US! LET ME—LET ME CONNECT YOU.
WHAT THE—?! THIS IS OUTRAGEOUS! I NEED BETTER HELP.
SECONDED! YOU SERIOUSLY NEED HELP!
OH! HANDSOME AND WITTY. WE COULD HAVE ACCOMPLISHED SO MUCH TOGETHER, MY DEAR BOY!
IT'S A SHAME YOU'RE NOT GOING TO MAKE IT TO THE SHOW. CRITICS SAY IT'S TO DIE FOR.

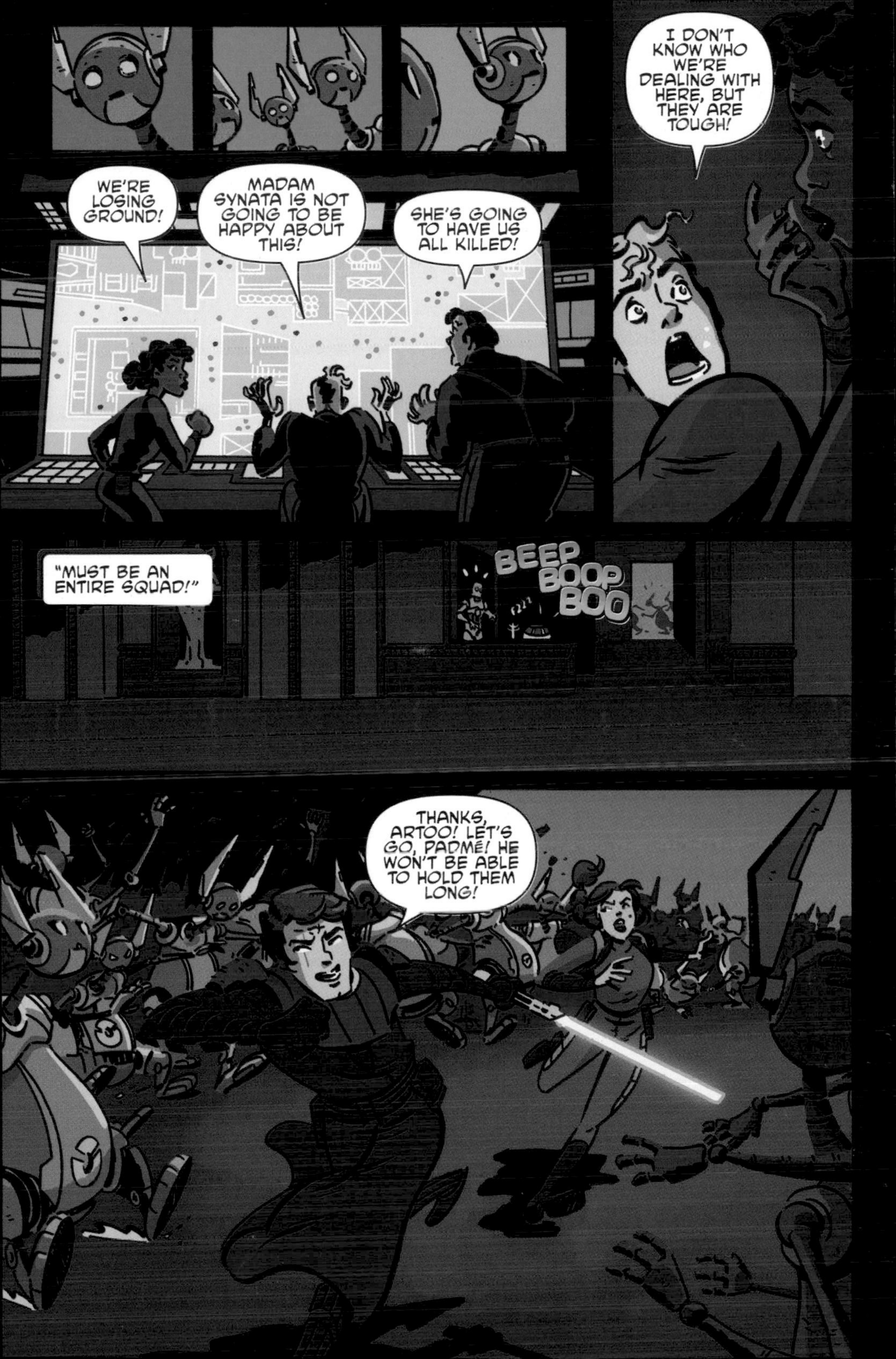

I DON'T KNOW WHO WE'RE DEALING WITH HERE, BUT THEY ARE TOUGH!
WE'RE LOSING GROUND!
MADAM SYNATA IS NOT GOING TO BE HAPPY ABOUT THIS!
SHE'S GOING TO HAVE US ALL KILLED!
"MUST BE AN ENTIRE SQUAD!"
BEEP BOOP BOO
THANKS, ARTOO! LET'S GO, PADMÉ! HE WON'T BE ABLE TO HOLD THEM LONG!

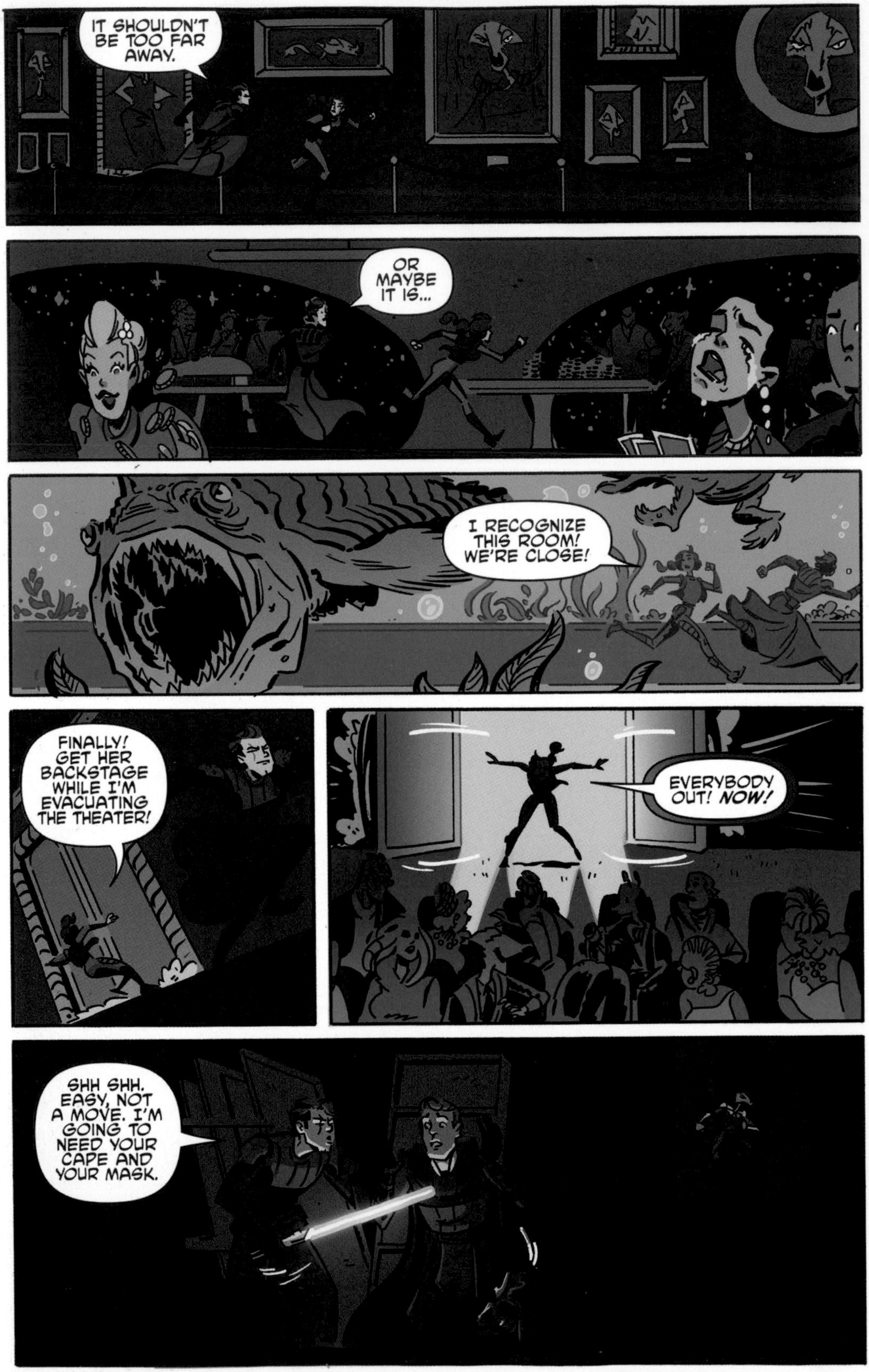
IT SHOULDN'T BE TOO FAR AWAY.
OR MAYBE IT IS...
I RECOGNIZE THIS ROOM! WE'RE CLOSE!
FINALLY! GET HER BACKSTAGE WHILE I'M EVACUATING THE THEATER!
EVERYBODY OUT! NOW!
SHH SHH. EASY, NOT A MOVE. I'M GOING TO NEED YOUR CAPE AND YOUR MASK.

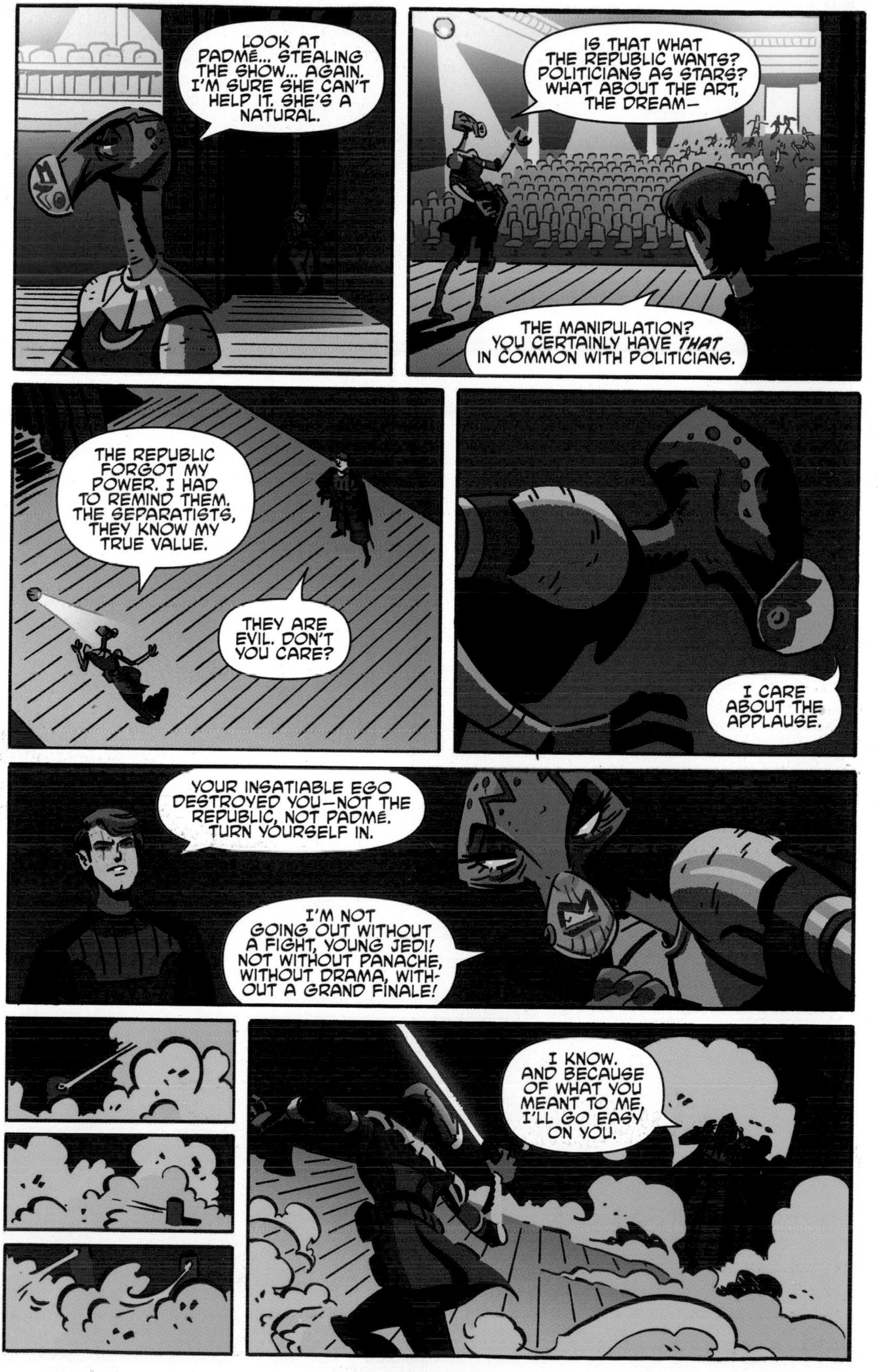
LOOK AT PADMÉ... STEALING THE SHOW... AGAIN. I'M SURE SHE CAN'T HELP IT. SHE'S A NATURAL.
IS THAT WHAT THE REPUBLIC WANTS? POLITICIANS AS STARS? WHAT ABOUT THE ART, THE DREAM—
THE MANIPULATION? YOU CERTAINLY HAVE *THAT* IN COMMON WITH POLITICIANS.
THE REPUBLIC FORGOT MY POWER. I HAD TO REMIND THEM. THE SEPARATISTS, THEY KNOW MY TRUE VALUE.
THEY ARE EVIL. DON'T YOU CARE?
I CARE ABOUT THE APPLAUSE.
YOUR INSATIABLE EGO DESTROYED YOU—NOT THE REPUBLIC, NOT PADMÉ. TURN YOURSELF IN.
I'M NOT GOING OUT WITHOUT A FIGHT, YOUNG JEDI! NOT WITHOUT PANACHE, WITHOUT DRAMA, WITHOUT A GRAND FINALE!
I KNOW. AND BECAUSE OF WHAT YOU MEANT TO ME, I'LL GO EASY ON YOU.

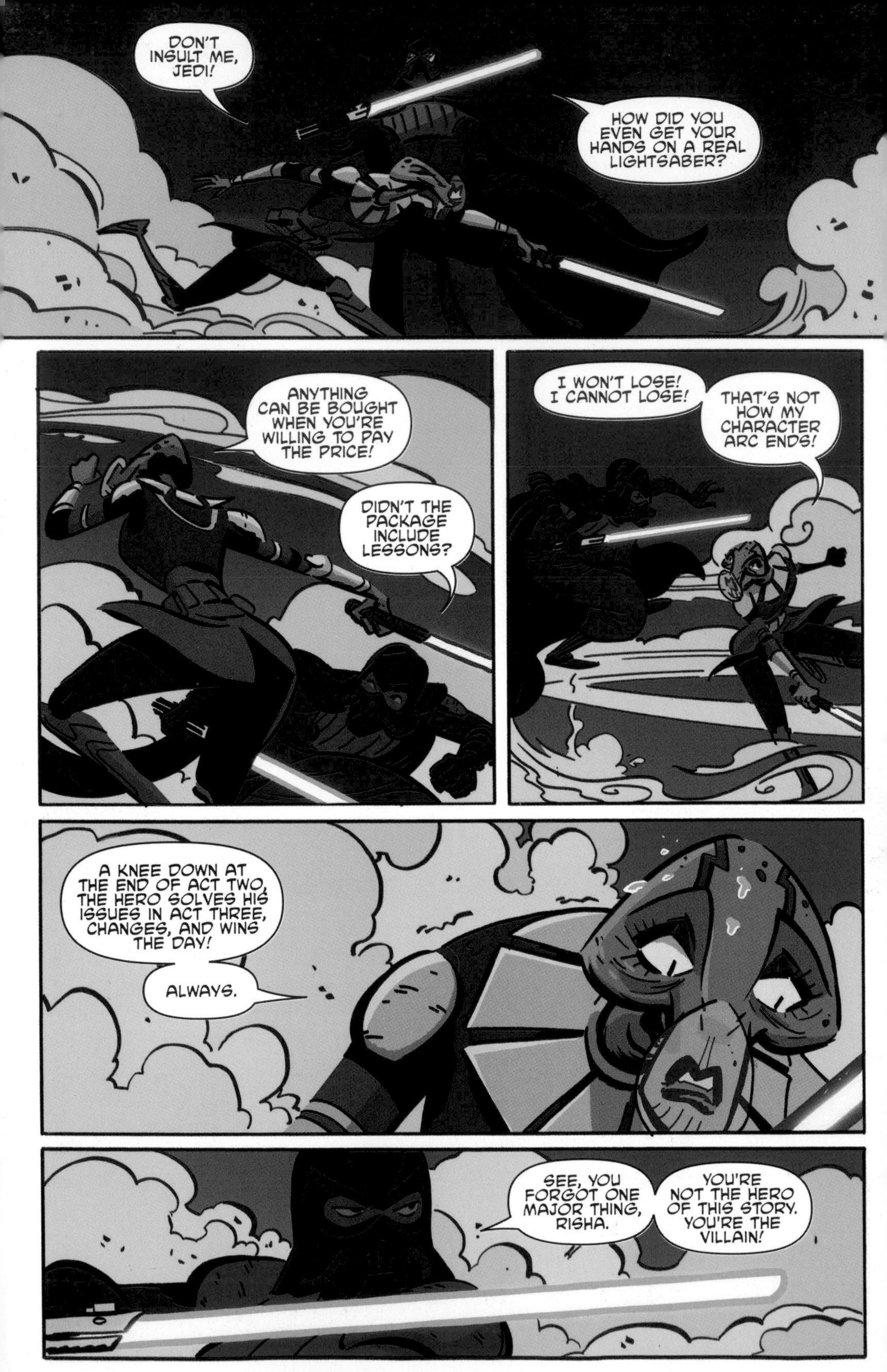
DON'T INSULT ME, JEDI!
HOW DID YOU EVEN GET YOUR HANDS ON A REAL LIGHTSABER?
ANYTHING CAN BE BOUGHT WHEN YOU'RE WILLING TO PAY THE PRICE!
DIDN'T THE PACKAGE INCLUDE LESSONS?
I WON'T LOSE! I CANNOT LOSE!
THAT'S NOT HOW MY CHARACTER ARC ENDS!
A KNEE DOWN AT THE END OF ACT TWO, THE HERO SOLVES HIS ISSUES IN ACT THREE, CHANGES, AND WINS THE DAY!
ALWAYS.
SEE, YOU FORGOT ONE MAJOR THING, RISHA.
YOU'RE NOT THE HERO OF THIS STORY. YOU'RE THE VILLAIN!

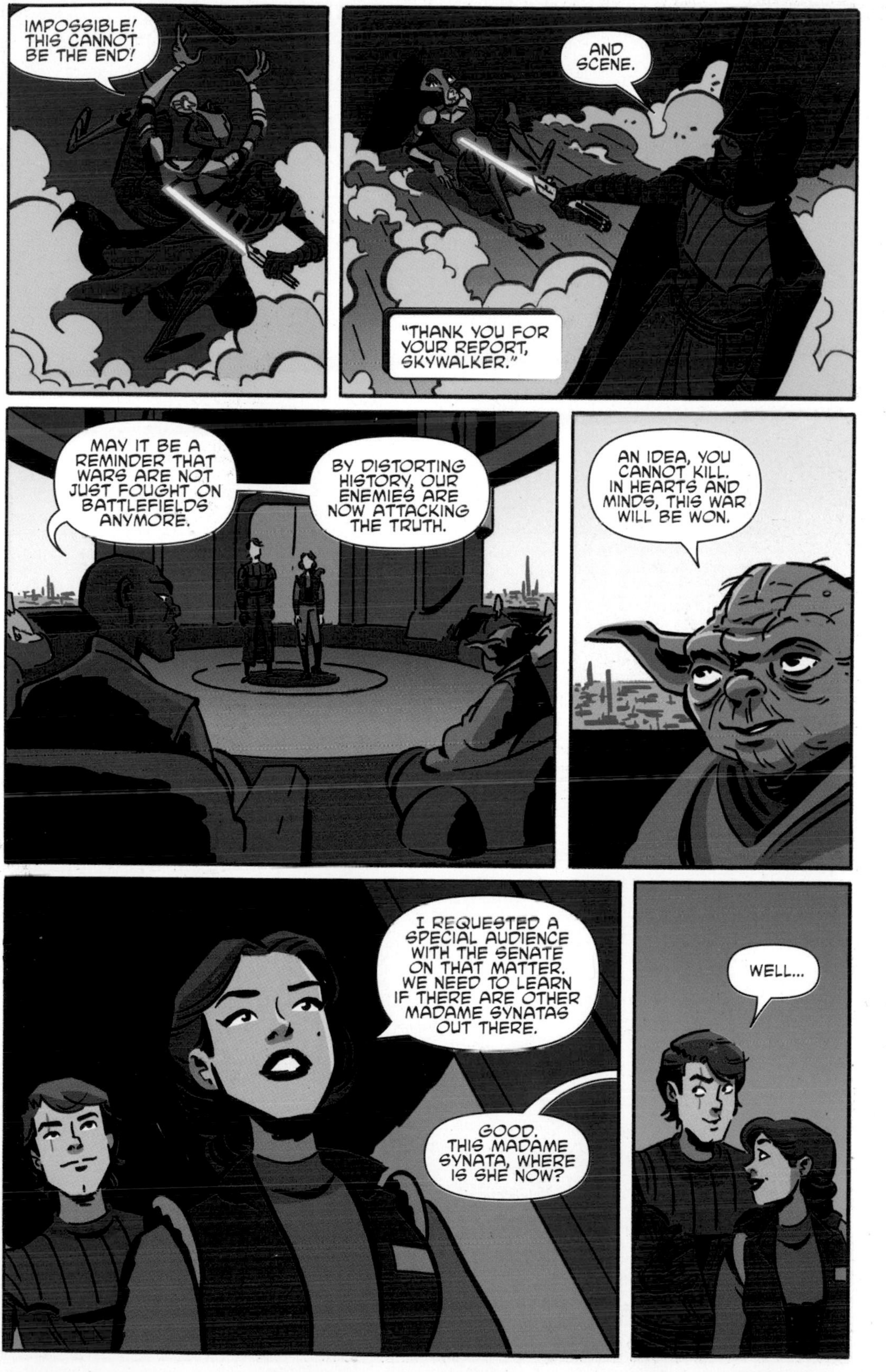
IMPOSSIBLE! THIS CANNOT BE THE END!
AND SCENE.
"THANK YOU FOR YOUR REPORT, SKYWALKER."
MAY IT BE A REMINDER THAT WARS ARE NOT JUST FOUGHT ON BATTLEFIELDS ANYMORE.
BY DISTORTING HISTORY, OUR ENEMIES ARE NOW ATTACKING THE TRUTH.
AN IDEA, YOU CANNOT KILL. IN HEARTS AND MINDS, THIS WAR WILL BE WON.
I REQUESTED A SPECIAL AUDIENCE WITH THE SENATE ON THAT MATTER. WE NEED TO LEARN IF THERE ARE OTHER MADAME SYNATAS OUT THERE.
GOOD. THIS MADAME SYNATA, WHERE IS SHE NOW?
WELL...

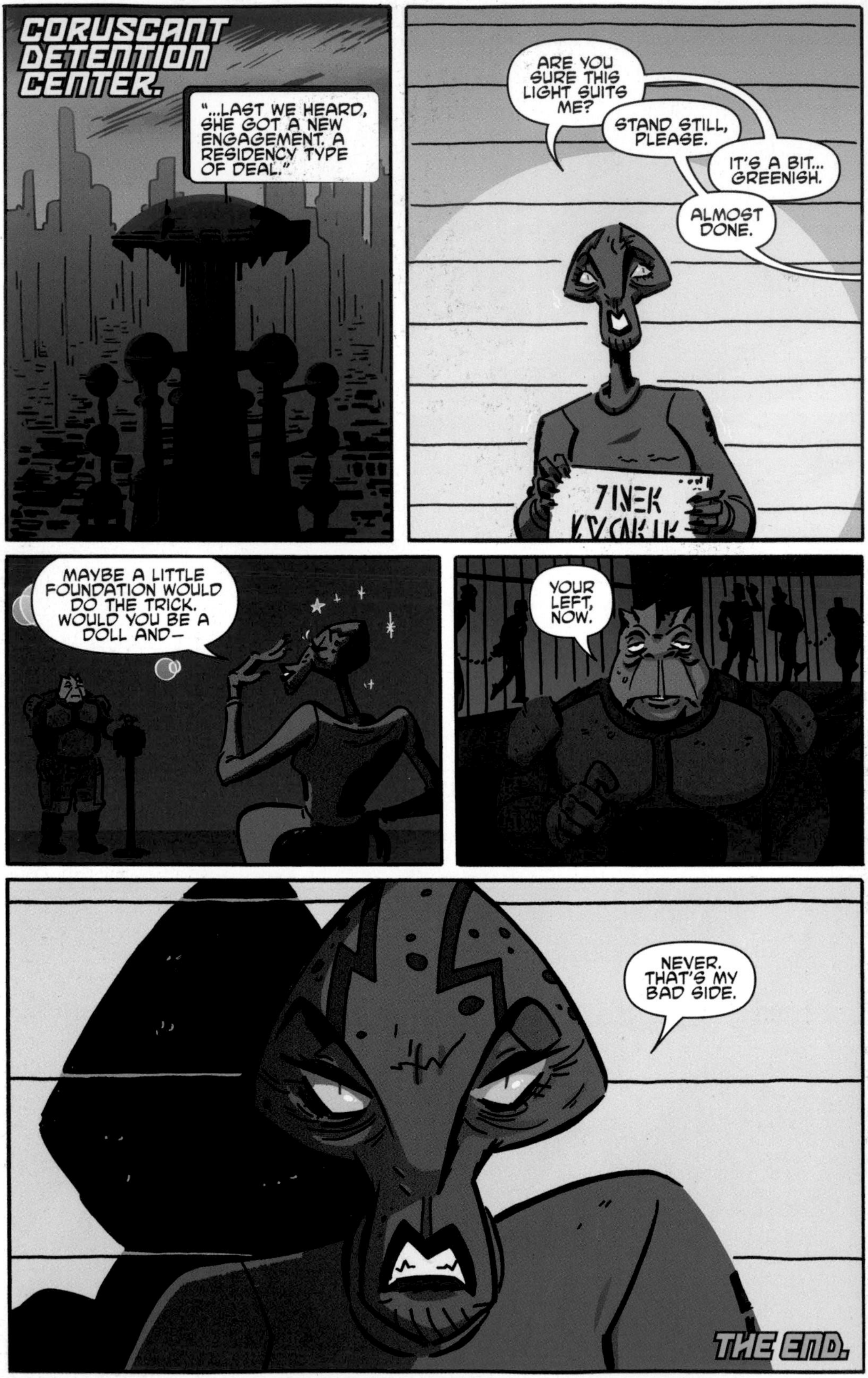
CORUSCANT DETENTION CENTER.
"...LAST WE HEARD, SHE GOT A NEW ENGAGEMENT. A RESIDENCY TYPE OF DEAL."
ARE YOU SURE THIS LIGHT SUITS ME?
STAND STILL, PLEASE.
IT'S A BIT... GREENISH.
ALMOST DONE.
MAYBE A LITTLE FOUNDATION WOULD DO THE TRICK. WOULD YOU BE A DOLL AND—
YOUR LEFT, NOW.
NEVER. THAT'S MY BAD SIDE.
THE END.

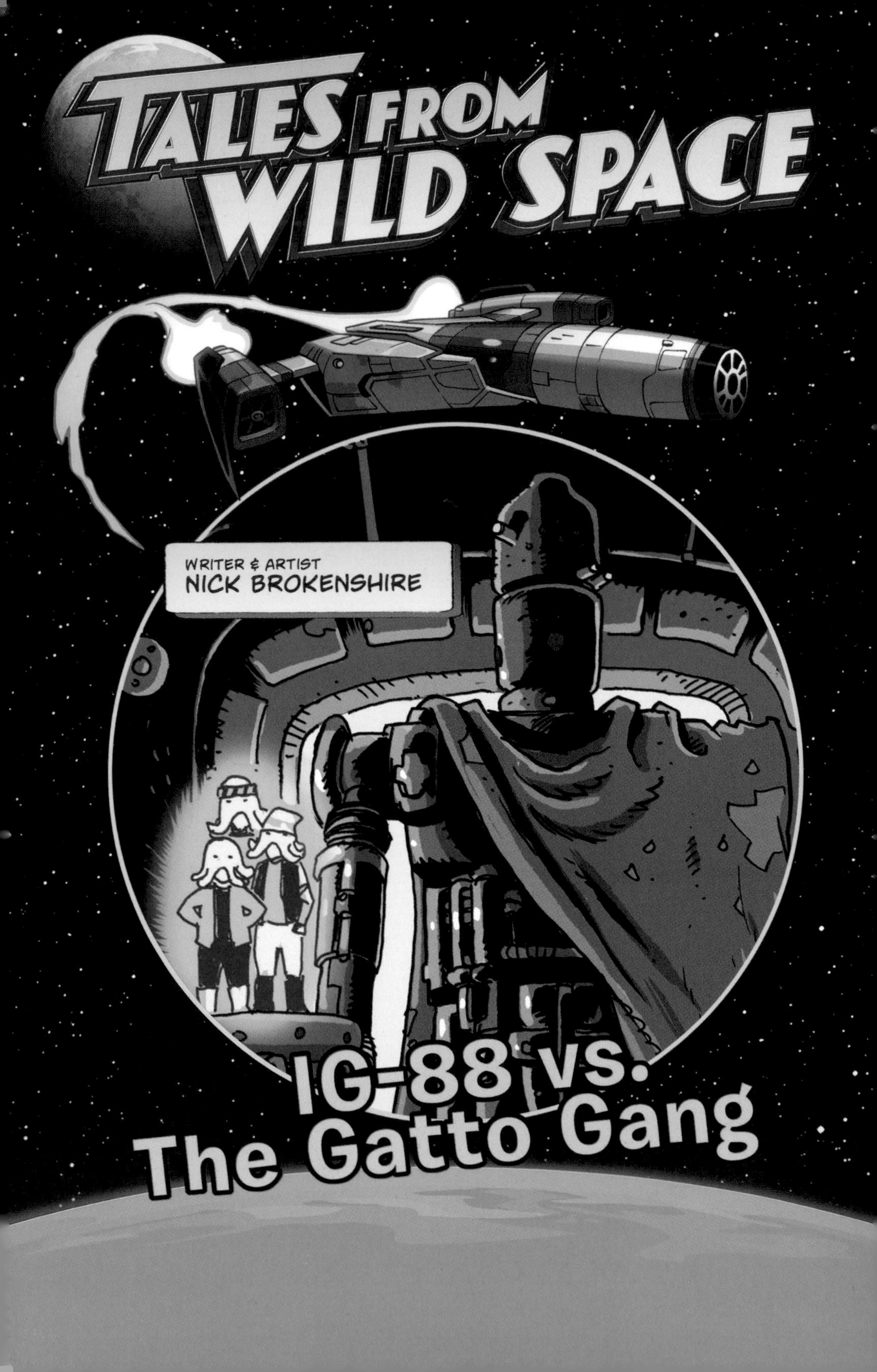
TALES FROM WILD SPACE
WRITER & ARTIST
NICK BROKENSHIRE
IG-88 vs. The Gatto Gang

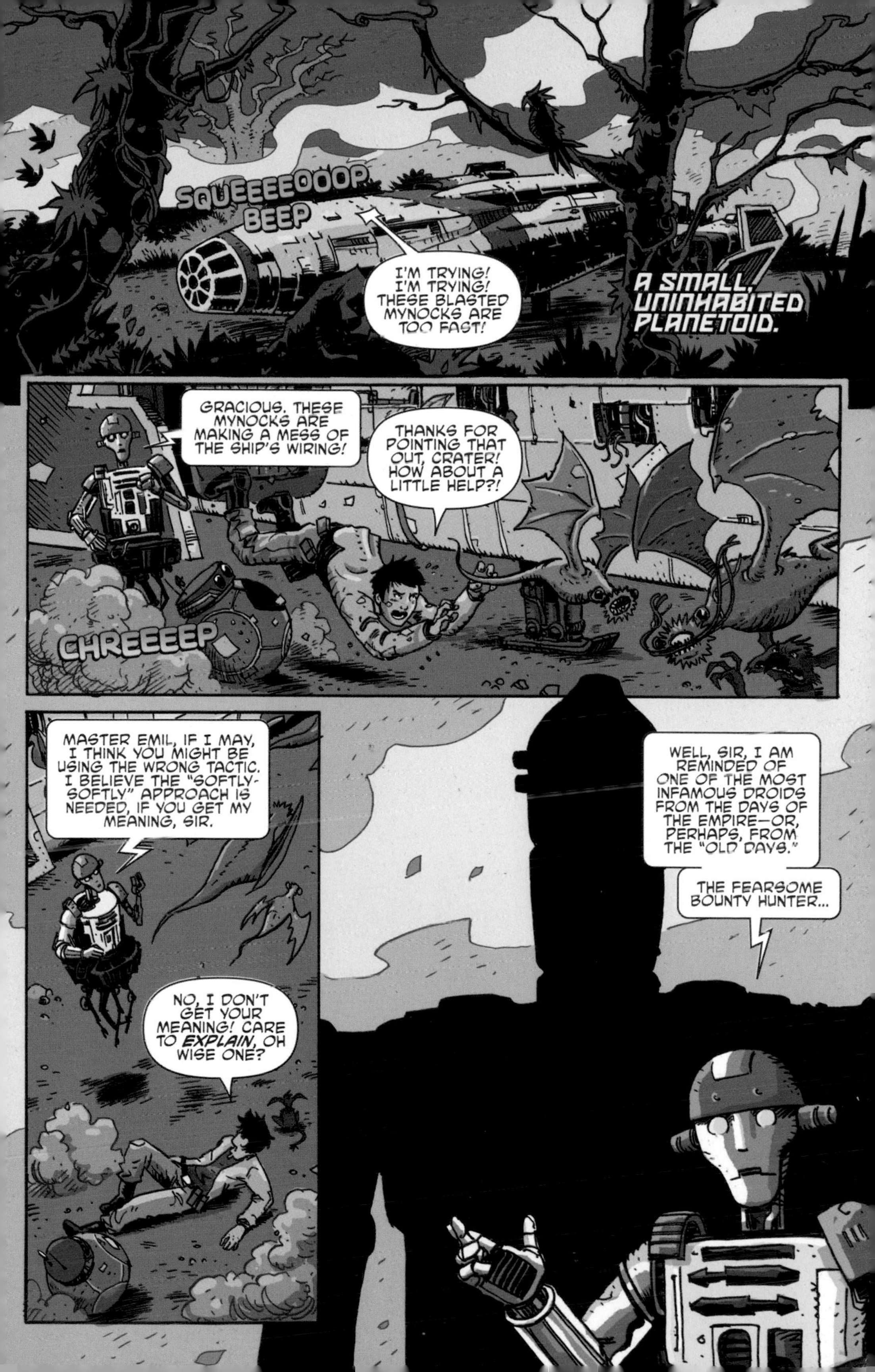
SQUEEEEOOOP
BEEP
I'M TRYING! I'M TRYING! THESE BLASTED MYNOCKS ARE TOO FAST!
A SMALL, UNINHABITED PLANETOID.
GRACIOUS. THESE MYNOCKS ARE MAKING A MESS OF THE SHIP'S WIRING!
THANKS FOR POINTING THAT OUT, CRATER! HOW ABOUT A LITTLE HELP?!
CHREEEEP
MASTER EMIL, IF I MAY, I THINK YOU MIGHT BE USING THE WRONG TACTIC. I BELIEVE THE "SOFTLY-SOFTLY" APPROACH IS NEEDED, IF YOU GET MY MEANING, SIR.
NO, I DON'T GET YOUR MEANING! CARE TO *EXPLAIN*, OH WISE ONE?
WELL, SIR, I AM REMINDED OF ONE OF THE MOST INFAMOUS DROIDS FROM THE DAYS OF THE EMPIRE—OR, PERHAPS, FROM THE "OLD DAYS."
THE FEARSOME BOUNTY HUNTER...

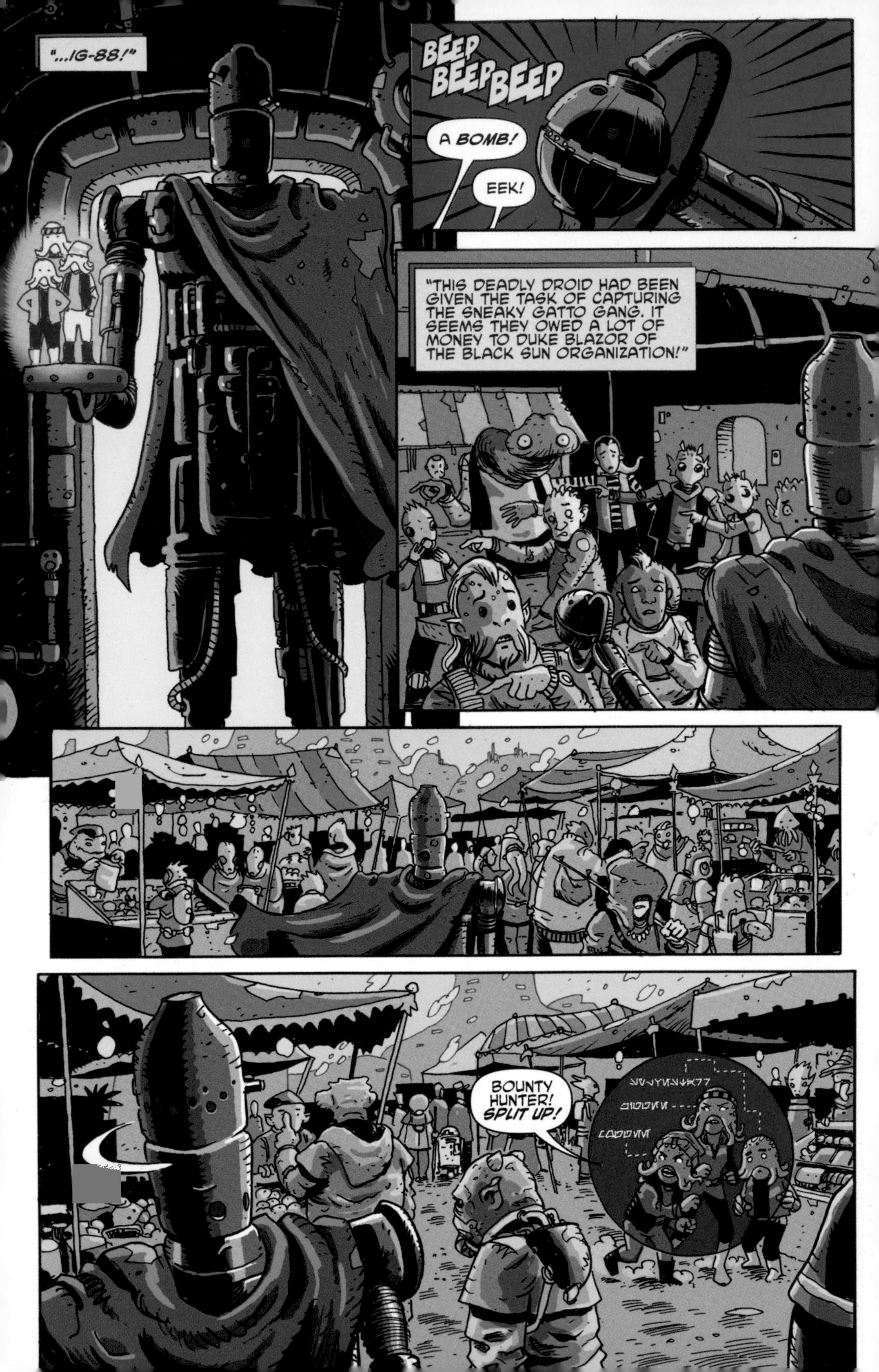
"...IG-88!"
BEEP BEEP BEEP
A BOMB!
EEK!
"THIS DEADLY DROID HAD BEEN GIVEN THE TASK OF CAPTURING THE SNEAKY GATTO GANG. IT SEEMS THEY OWED A LOT OF MONEY TO DUKE BLAZOR OF THE BLACK SUN ORGANIZATION!"
BOUNTY HUNTER! SPLIT UP!

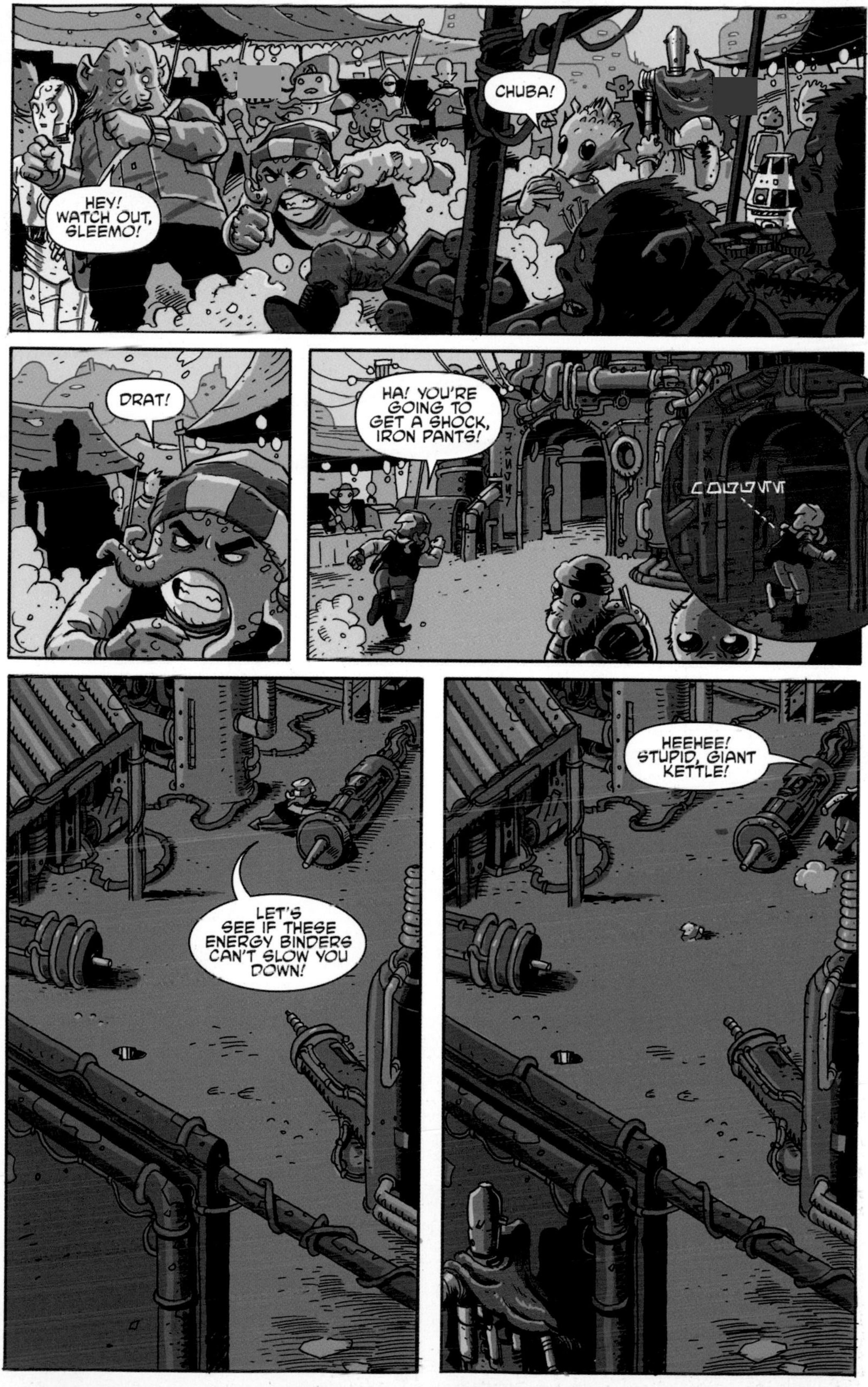
HEY! WATCH OUT, SLEEMO!
CHUBA!
DRAT!
HA! YOU'RE GOING TO GET A SHOCK, IRON PANTS!
LET'S SEE IF THESE ENERGY BINDERS CAN'T SLOW YOU DOWN!
HEEHEE! STUPID, GIANT KETTLE!

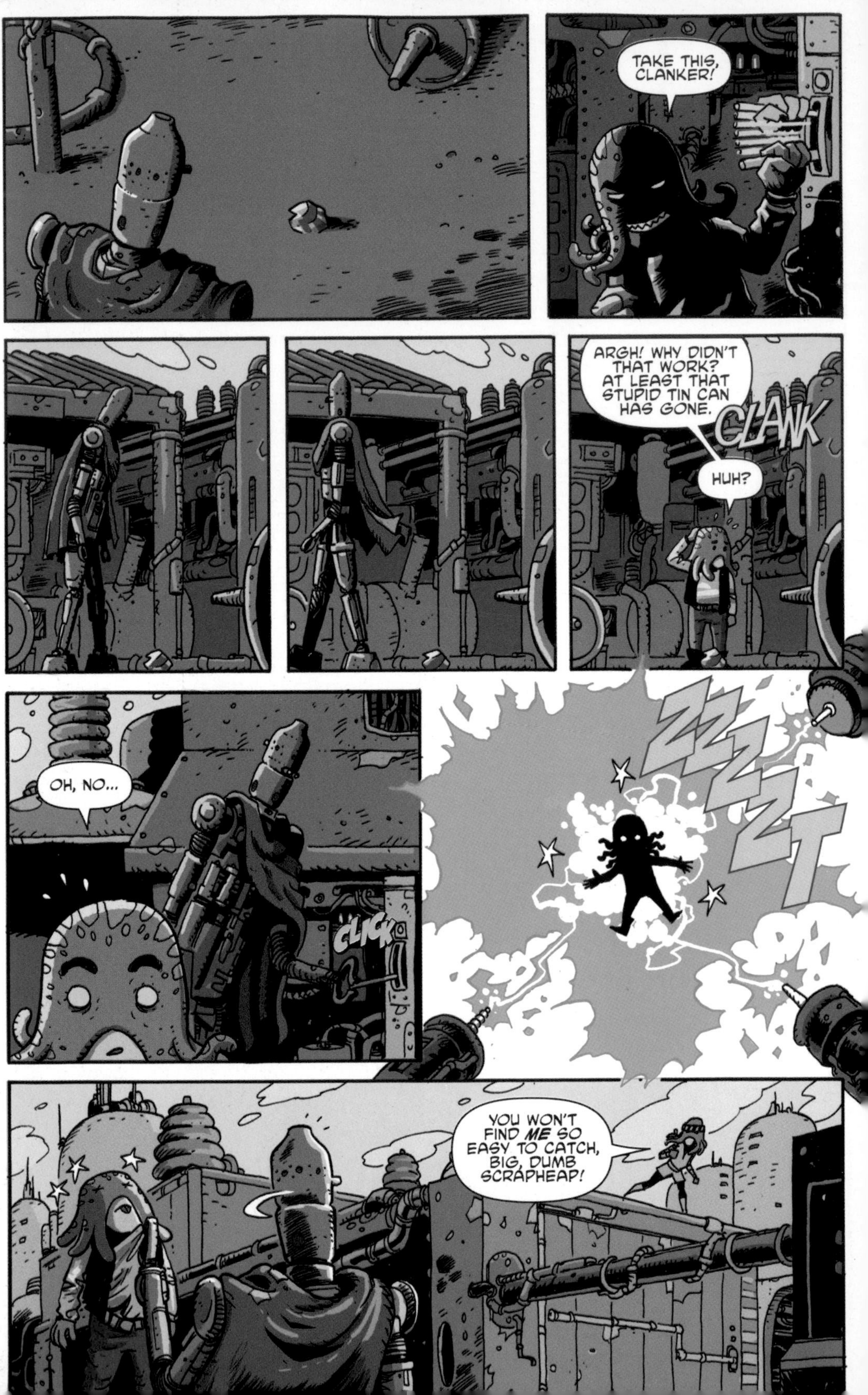
TAKE THIS, CLANKER!
ARGH! WHY DIDN'T THAT WORK? AT LEAST THAT STUPID TIN CAN HAS GONE.
CLANK
HUH?
OH, NO...
CLICK
ZZZZT
YOU WON'T FIND *ME* SO EASY TO CATCH, BIG, DUMB SCRAPHEAP!

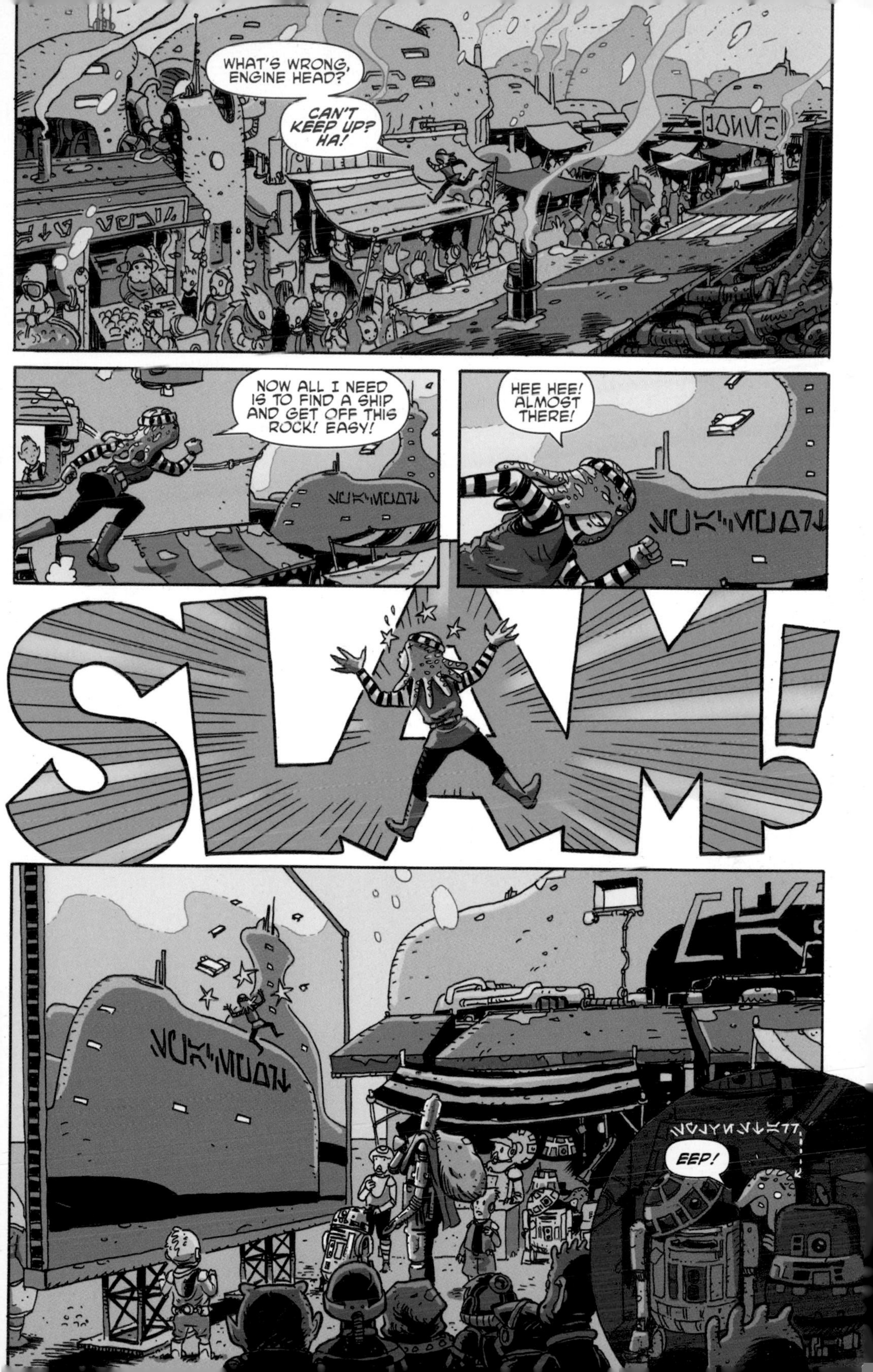
WHAT'S WRONG, ENGINE HEAD?
CAN'T KEEP UP? HA!
NOW ALL I NEED IS TO FIND A SHIP AND GET OFF THIS ROCK! EASY!
HEE HEE! ALMOST THERE!
SLAM!
EEP!

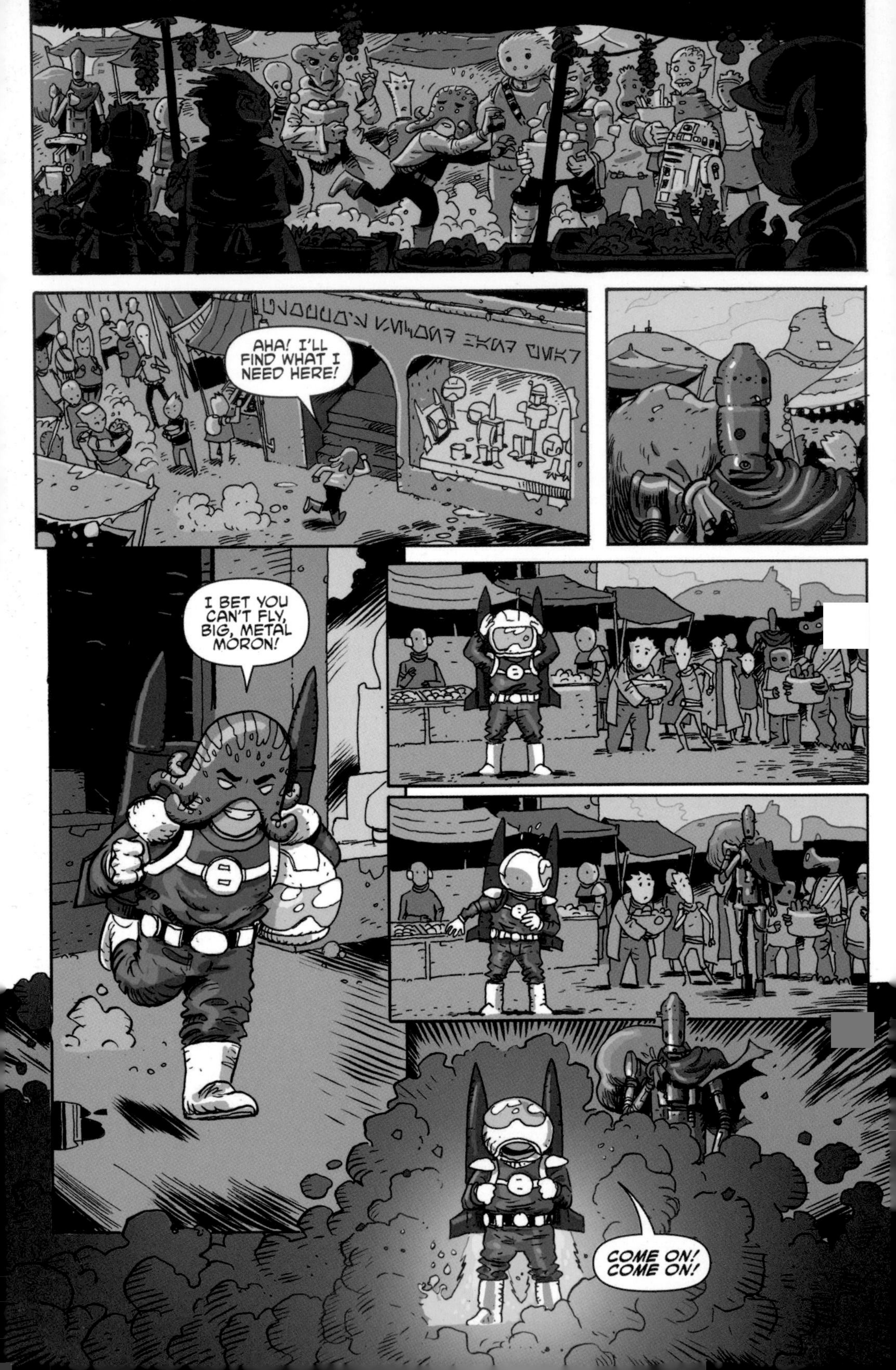
AHA! I'LL FIND WHAT I NEED HERE!
I BET YOU CAN'T FLY, BIG, METAL MORON!
COME ON! COME ON!

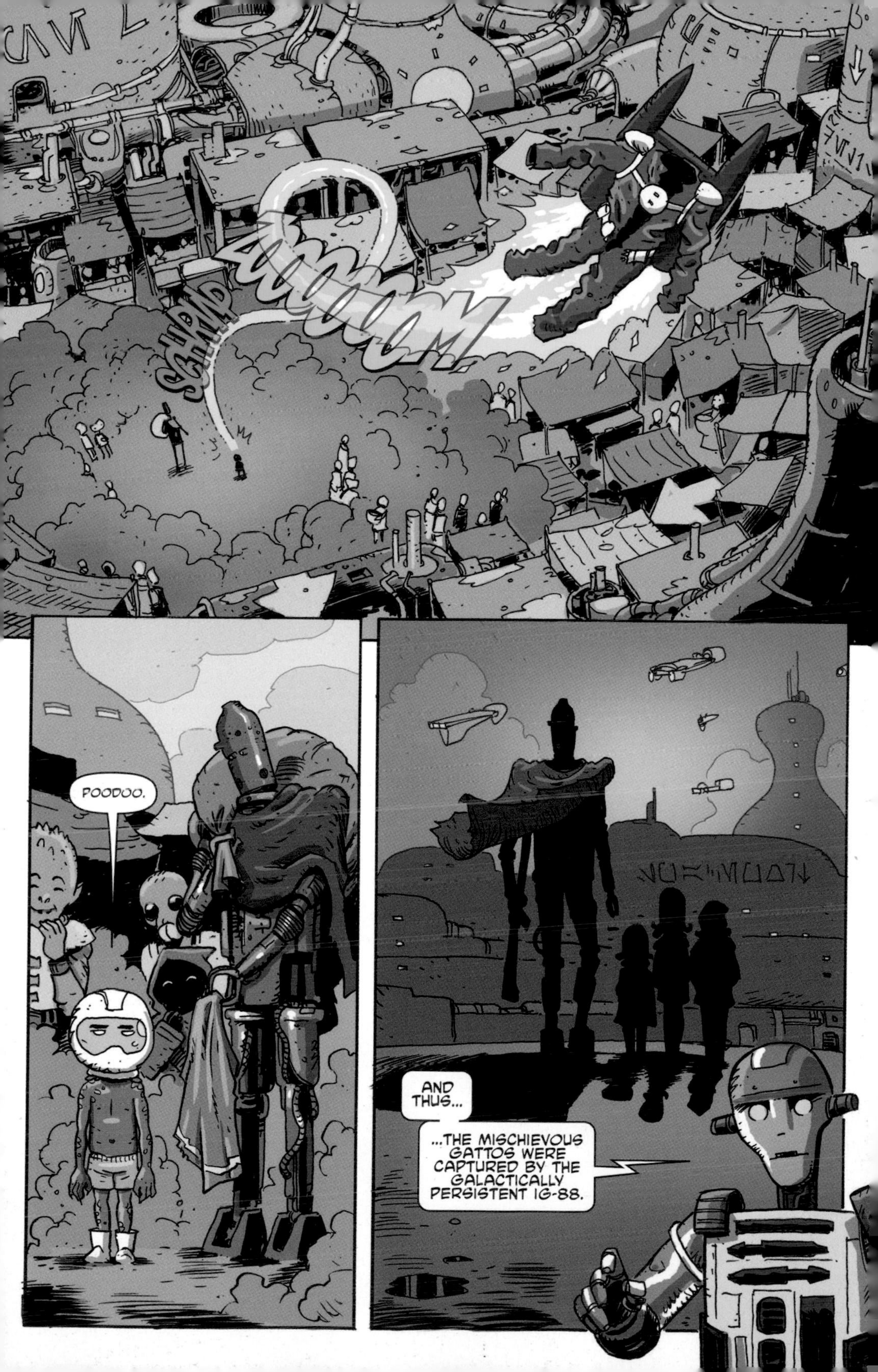
SCHRAP
ZOOOOOOOM
POODOO.
AND THUS...
...THE MISCHIEVOUS GATTOS WERE CAPTURED BY THE GALACTICALLY PERSISTENT IG-88.

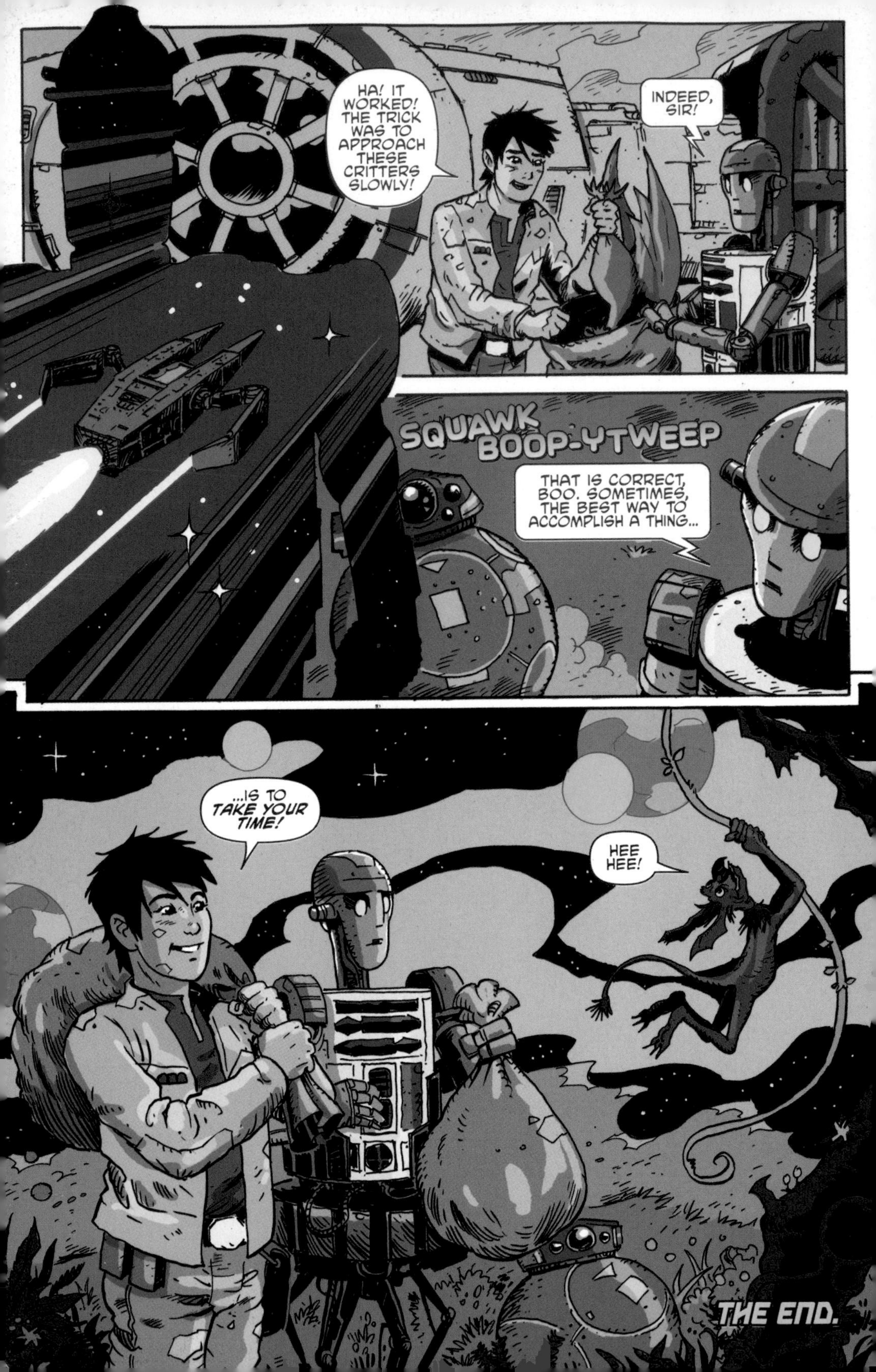
HA! IT WORKED! THE TRICK WAS TO APPROACH THESE CRITTERS SLOWLY!
INDEED, SIR!
SQUAWK
BOOP-YTWEEP
THAT IS CORRECT, BOO. SOMETIMES, THE BEST WAY TO ACCOMPLISH A THING...
...IS TO TAKE YOUR TIME!
HEE HEE!
THE END.

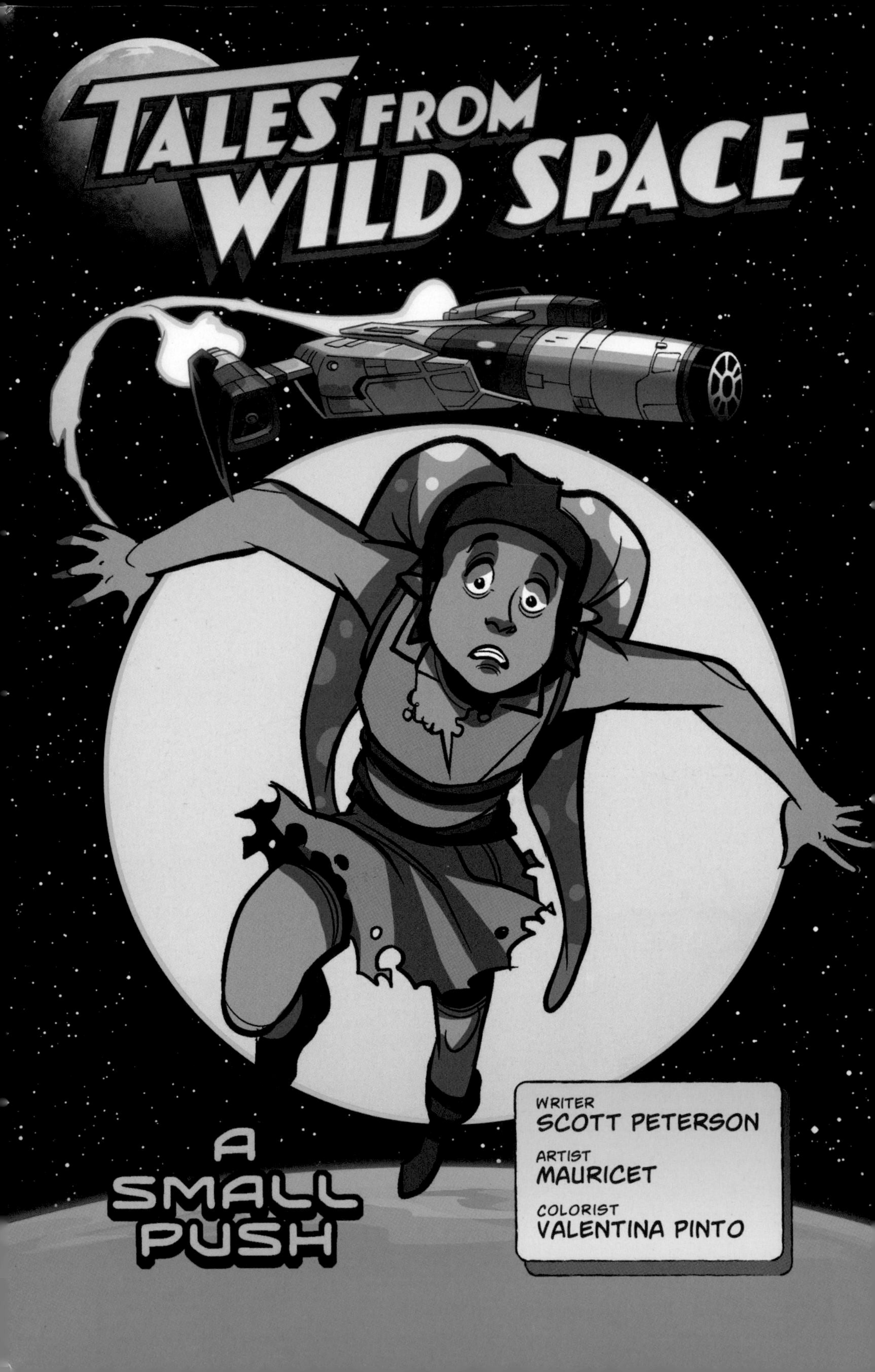
TALES FROM WILD SPACE
A SMALL PUSH
WRITER
SCOTT PETERSON
ARTIST
MAURICET
COLORIST
VALENTINA PINTO

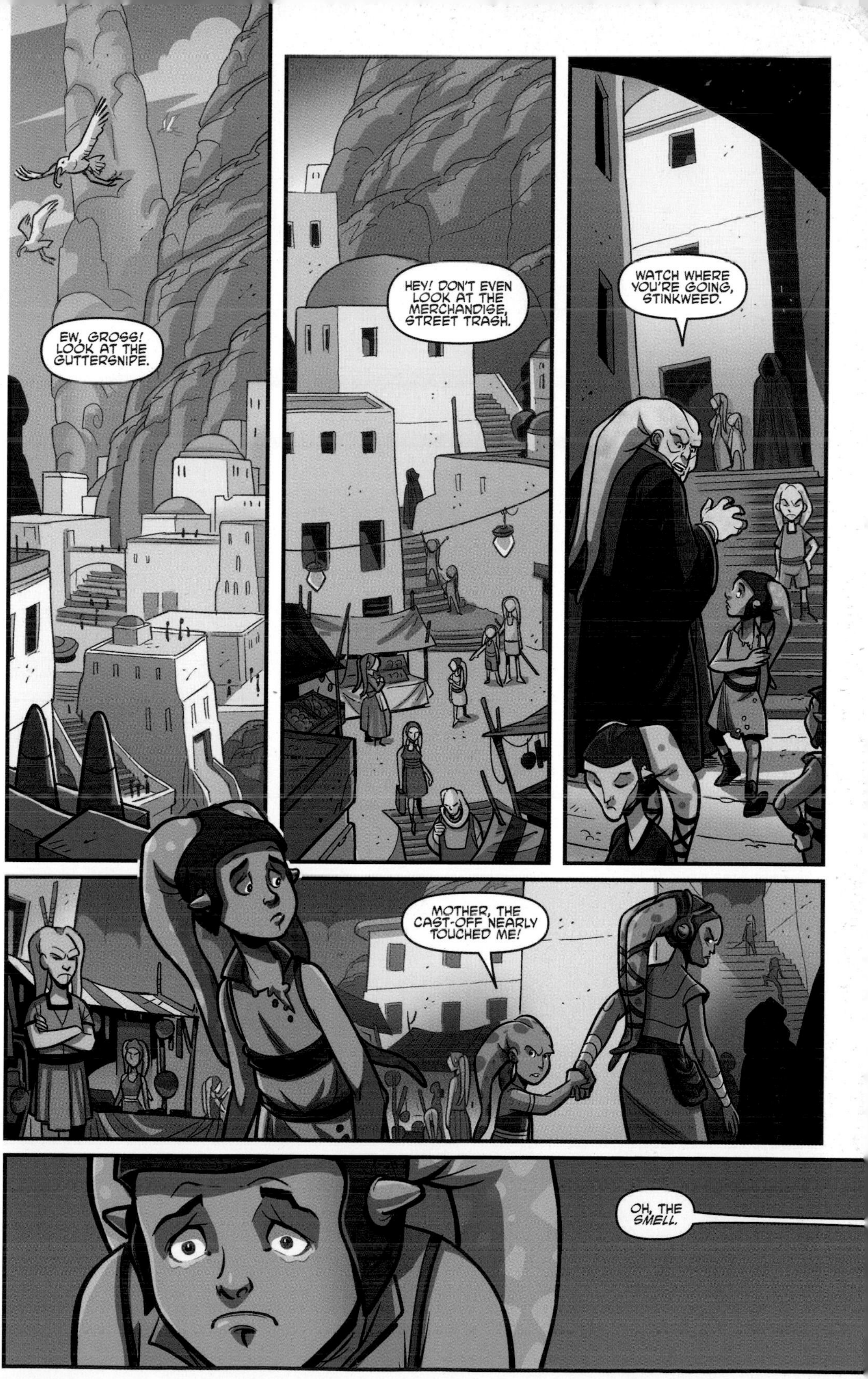
EW, GROSS! LOOK AT THE GUTTERSNIPE.
HEY! DON'T EVEN LOOK AT THE MERCHANDISE, STREET TRASH.
WATCH WHERE YOU'RE GOING, STINKWEED.
MOTHER, THE CAST-OFF NEARLY TOUCHED ME!
OH, THE SMELL.

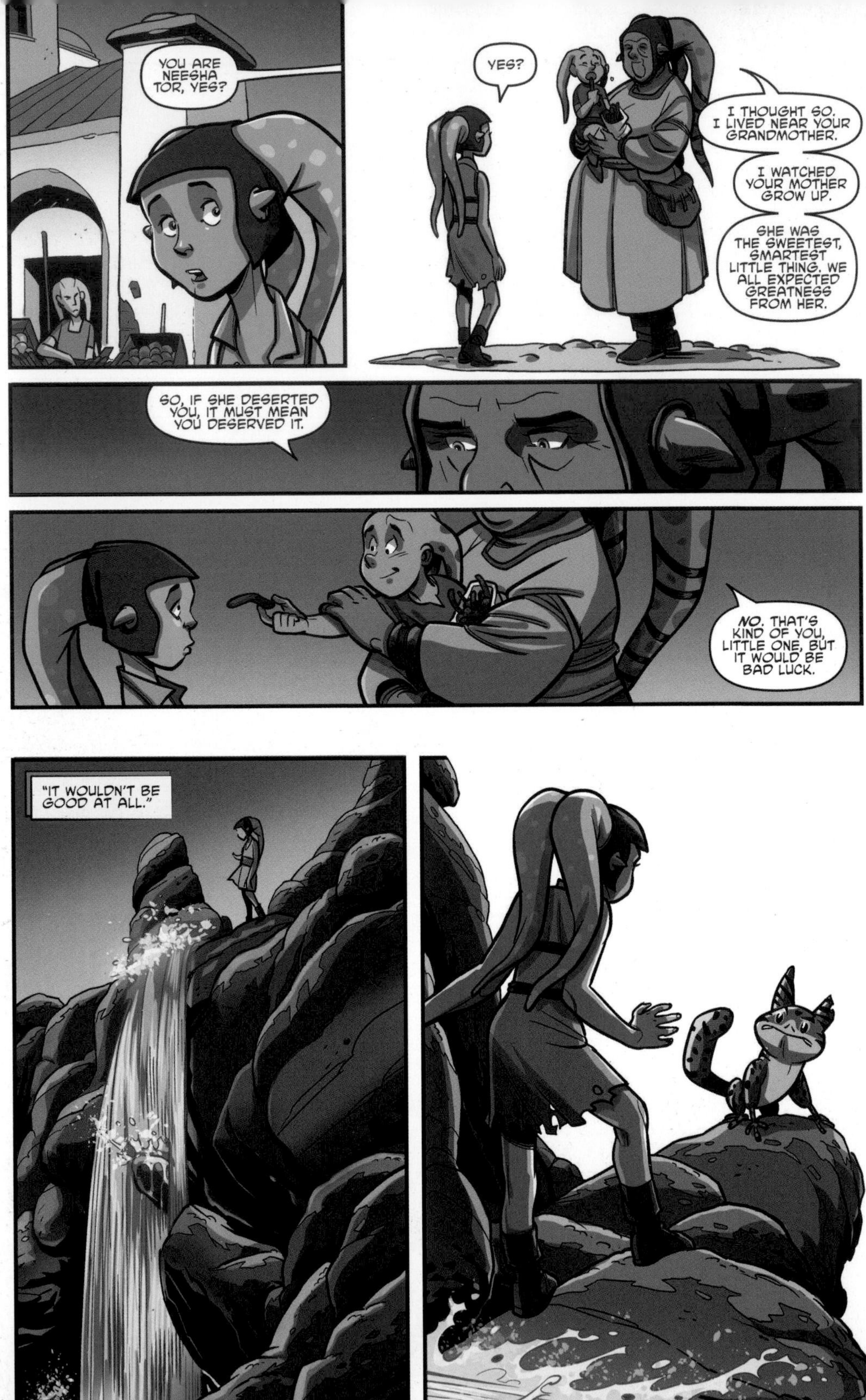
YOU ARE NEESHA TOR, YES?
YES?
I THOUGHT SO. I LIVED NEAR YOUR GRANDMOTHER.
I WATCHED YOUR MOTHER GROW UP.
SHE WAS THE SWEETEST, SMARTEST LITTLE THING. WE ALL EXPECTED GREATNESS FROM HER.
SO, IF SHE DESERTED YOU, IT MUST MEAN YOU DESERVED IT.
NO. THAT'S KIND OF YOU, LITTLE ONE, BUT IT WOULD BE BAD LUCK.
"IT WOULDN'T BE GOOD AT ALL."

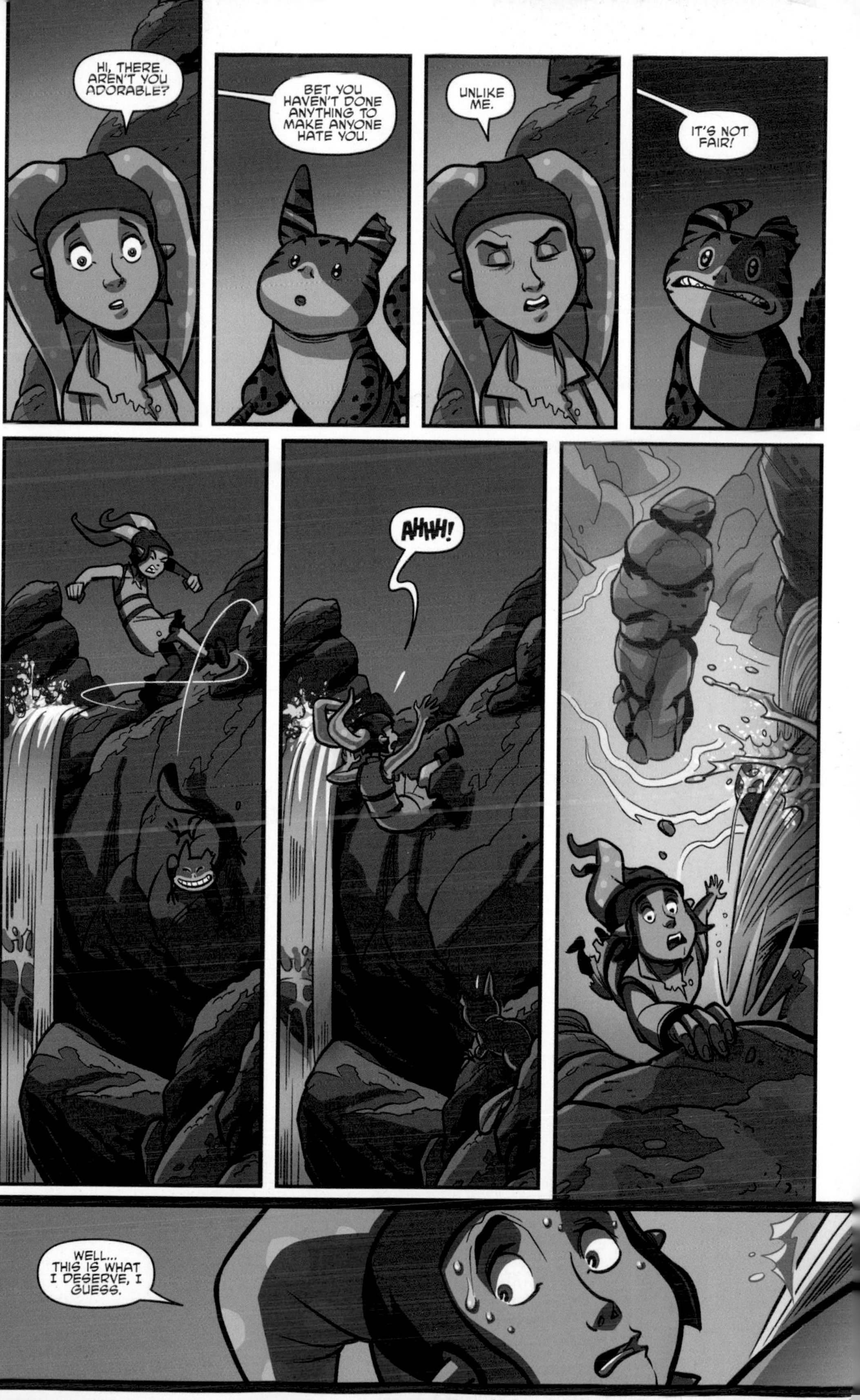
HI, THERE. AREN'T YOU ADORABLE?
BET YOU HAVEN'T DONE ANYTHING TO MAKE ANYONE HATE YOU.
UNLIKE ME.
IT'S NOT FAIR!
AHHH!
WELL... THIS IS WHAT I DESERVE, I GUESS.

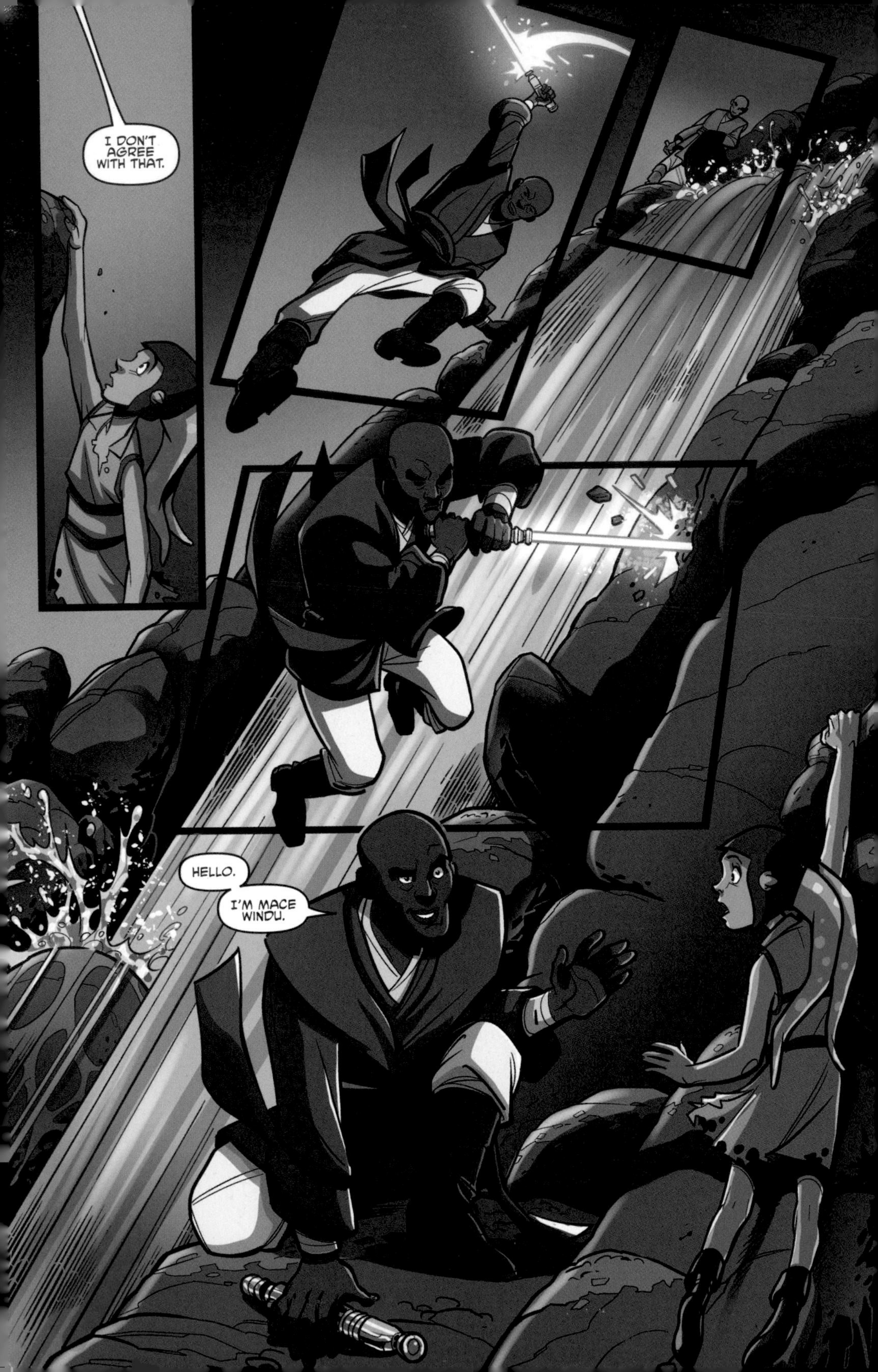
I DON'T AGREE WITH THAT.
HELLO.
I'M MACE WINDU.

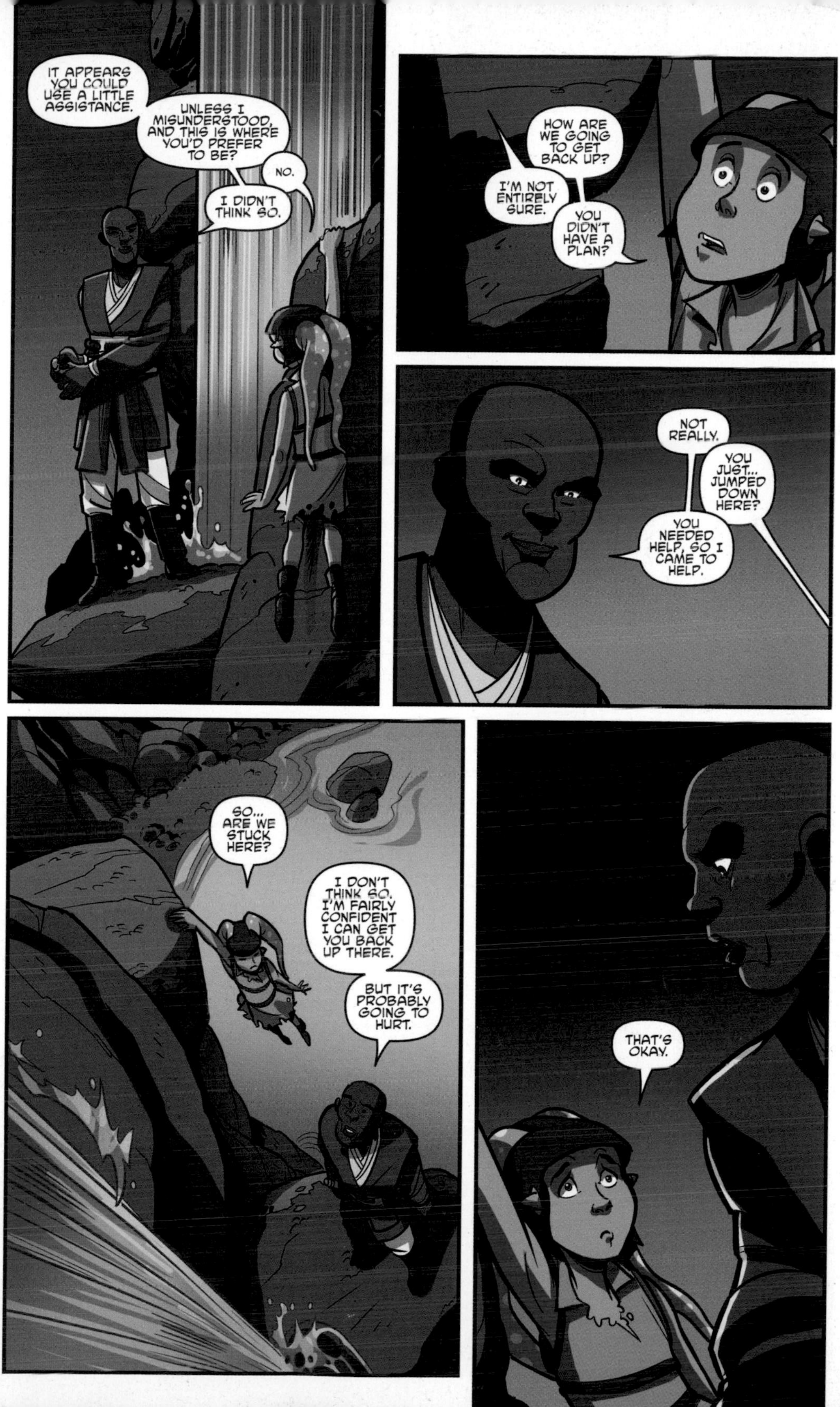

IT APPEARS YOU COULD USE A LITTLE ASSISTANCE.
UNLESS I MISUNDERSTOOD, AND THIS IS WHERE YOU'D PREFER TO BE?
NO.
I DIDN'T THINK SO.
HOW ARE WE GOING TO GET BACK UP?
I'M NOT ENTIRELY SURE.
YOU DIDN'T HAVE A PLAN?
NOT REALLY.
YOU JUST... JUMPED DOWN HERE?
YOU NEEDED HELP, SO I CAME TO HELP.
SO... ARE WE STUCK HERE?
I DON'T THINK SO. I'M FAIRLY CONFIDENT I CAN GET YOU BACK UP THERE.
BUT IT'S PROBABLY GOING TO HURT.
THAT'S OKAY.

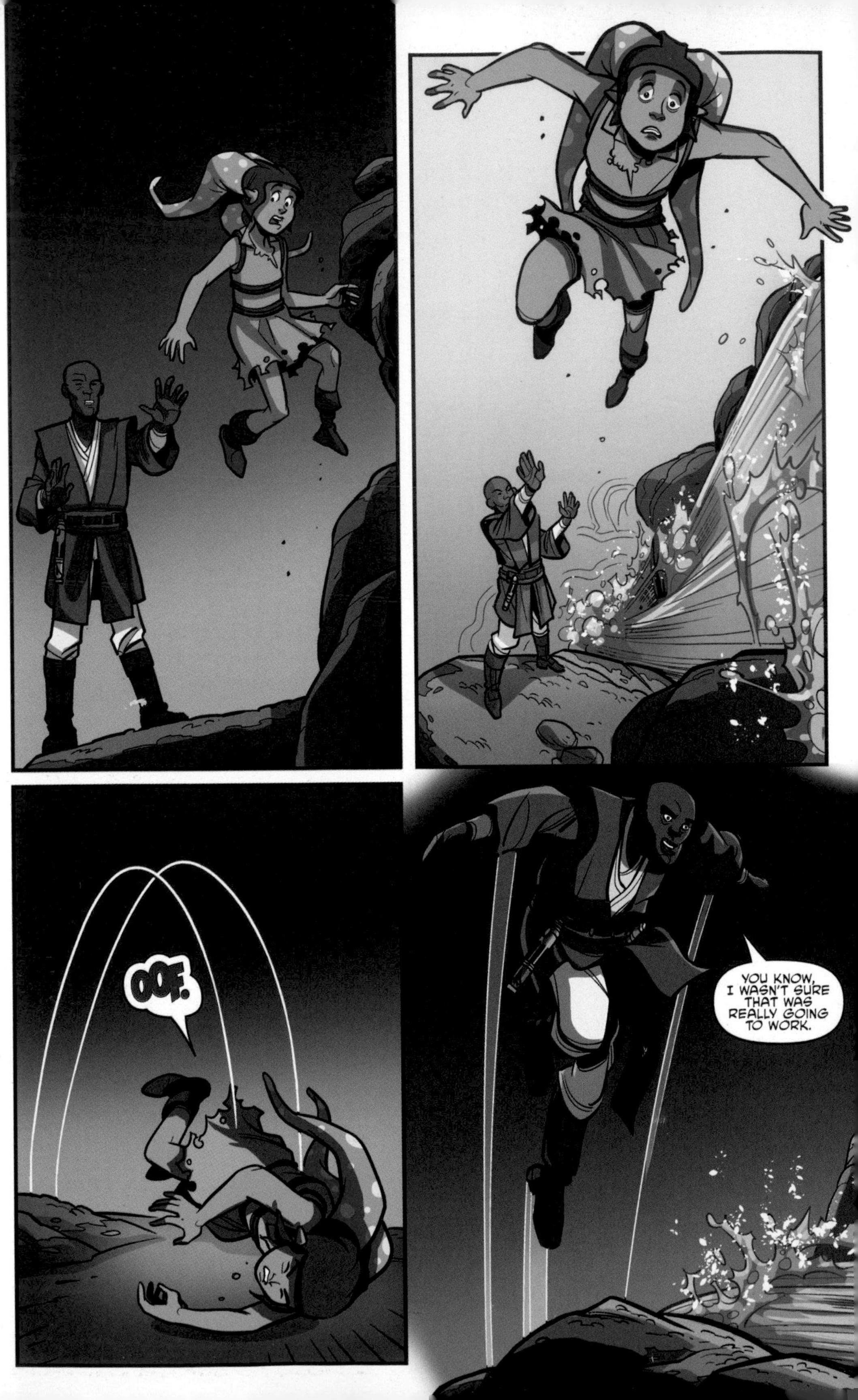
OOF.
YOU KNOW, I WASN'T SURE THAT WAS REALLY GOING TO WORK.

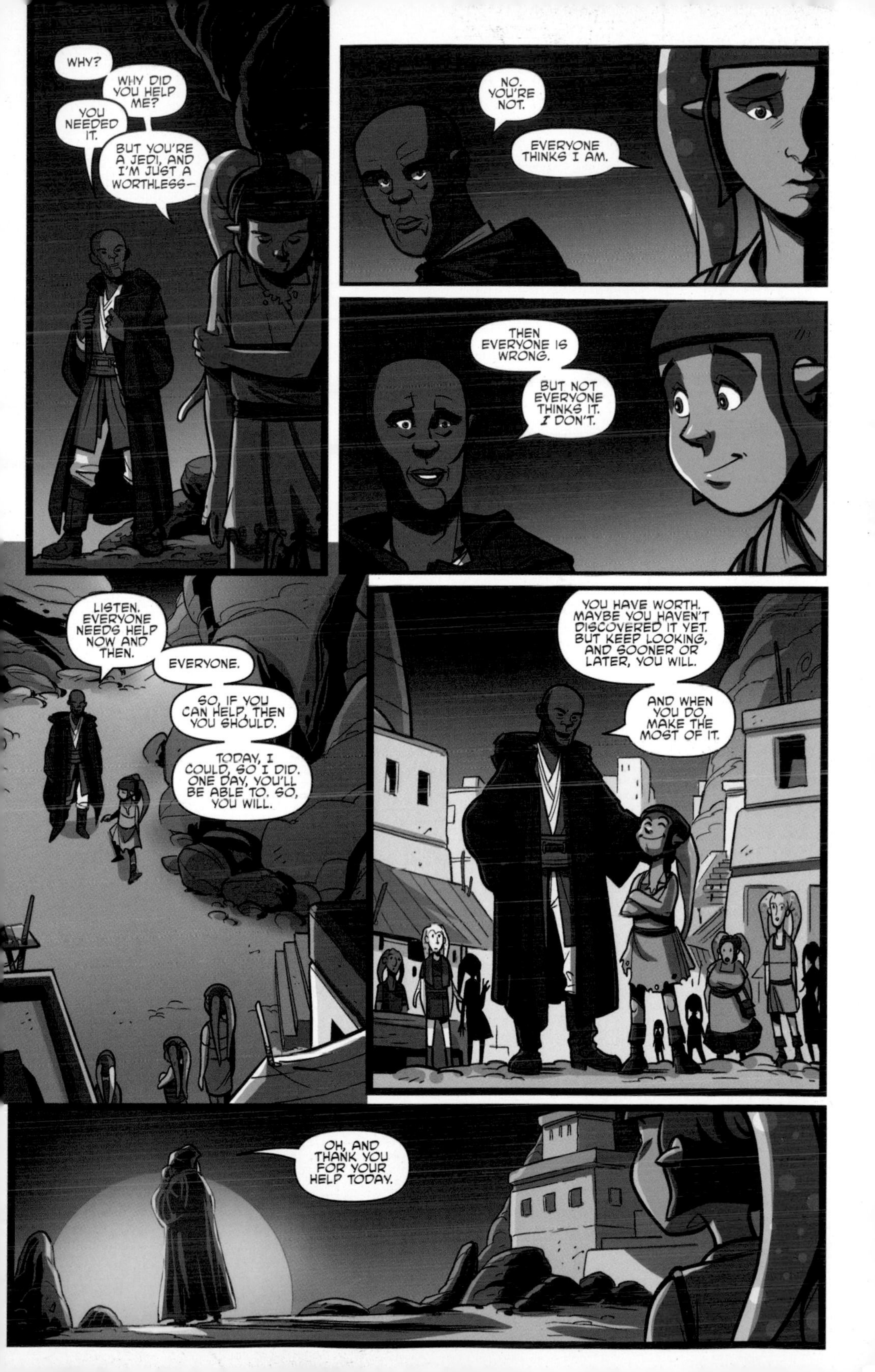
WHY?
WHY DID YOU HELP ME?
YOU NEEDED IT.
BUT YOU'RE A JEDI, AND I'M JUST A WORTHLESS—
NO. YOU'RE NOT.
EVERYONE THINKS I AM.
THEN EVERYONE IS WRONG.
BUT NOT EVERYONE THINKS IT. *I* DON'T.
LISTEN. EVERYONE NEEDS HELP NOW AND THEN.
EVERYONE.
SO, IF YOU CAN HELP, THEN YOU SHOULD.
TODAY, I COULD, SO I DID. ONE DAY, YOU'LL BE ABLE TO. SO, YOU WILL.
YOU HAVE WORTH. MAYBE YOU HAVEN'T DISCOVERED IT YET. BUT KEEP LOOKING, AND SOONER OR LATER, YOU WILL.
AND WHEN YOU DO, MAKE THE MOST OF IT.
OH, AND THANK YOU FOR YOUR HELP TODAY.

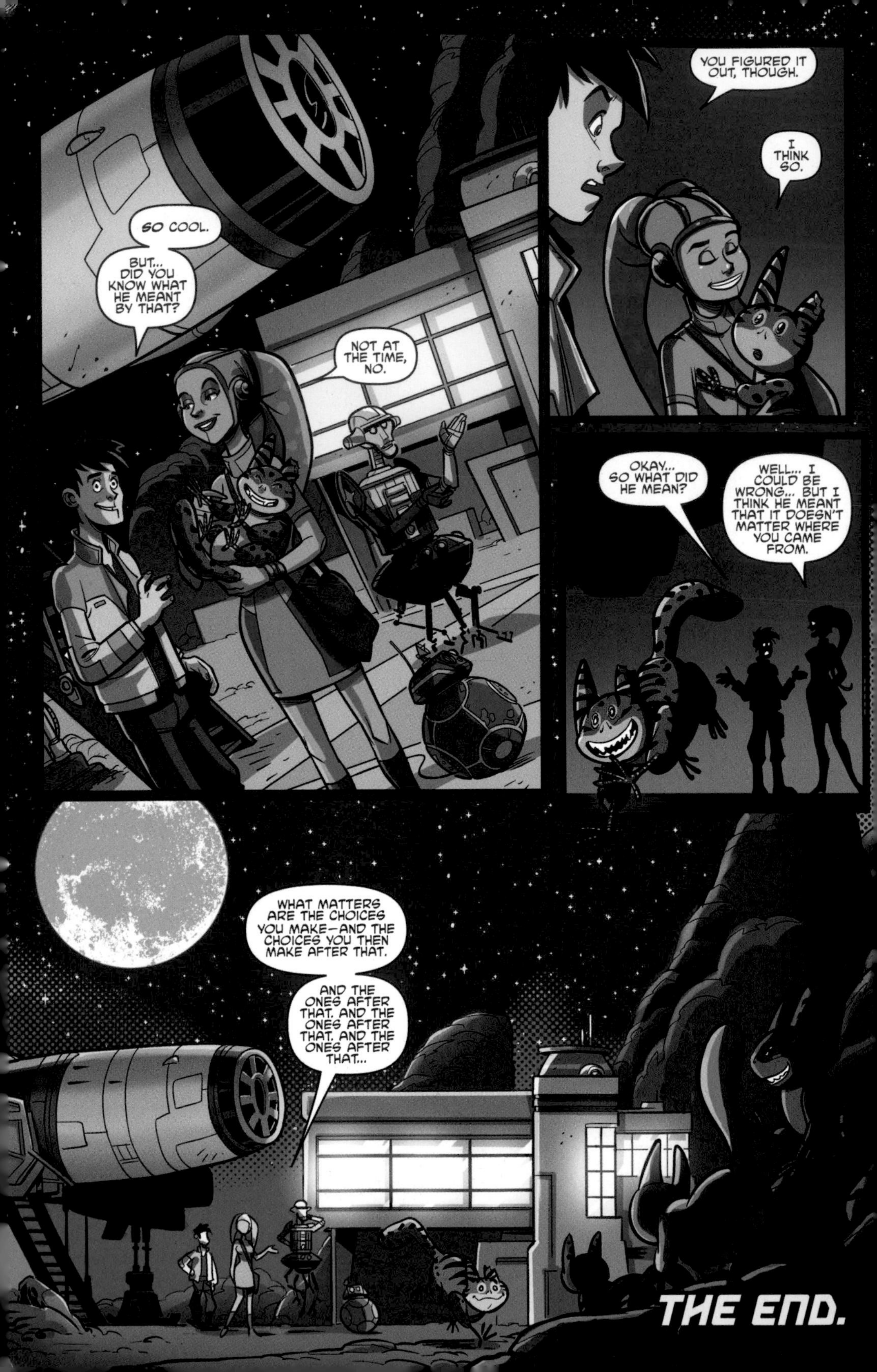
SO COOL.
BUT... DID YOU KNOW WHAT HE MEANT BY THAT?
NOT AT THE TIME, NO.
YOU FIGURED IT OUT, THOUGH.
I THINK SO.
OKAY... SO WHAT DID HE MEAN?
WELL... I COULD BE WRONG... BUT I THINK HE MEANT THAT IT DOESN'T MATTER WHERE YOU CAME FROM.
WHAT MATTERS ARE THE CHOICES YOU MAKE—AND THE CHOICES YOU THEN MAKE AFTER THAT.
AND THE ONES AFTER THAT. AND THE ONES AFTER THAT. AND THE ONES AFTER THAT...
THE END.

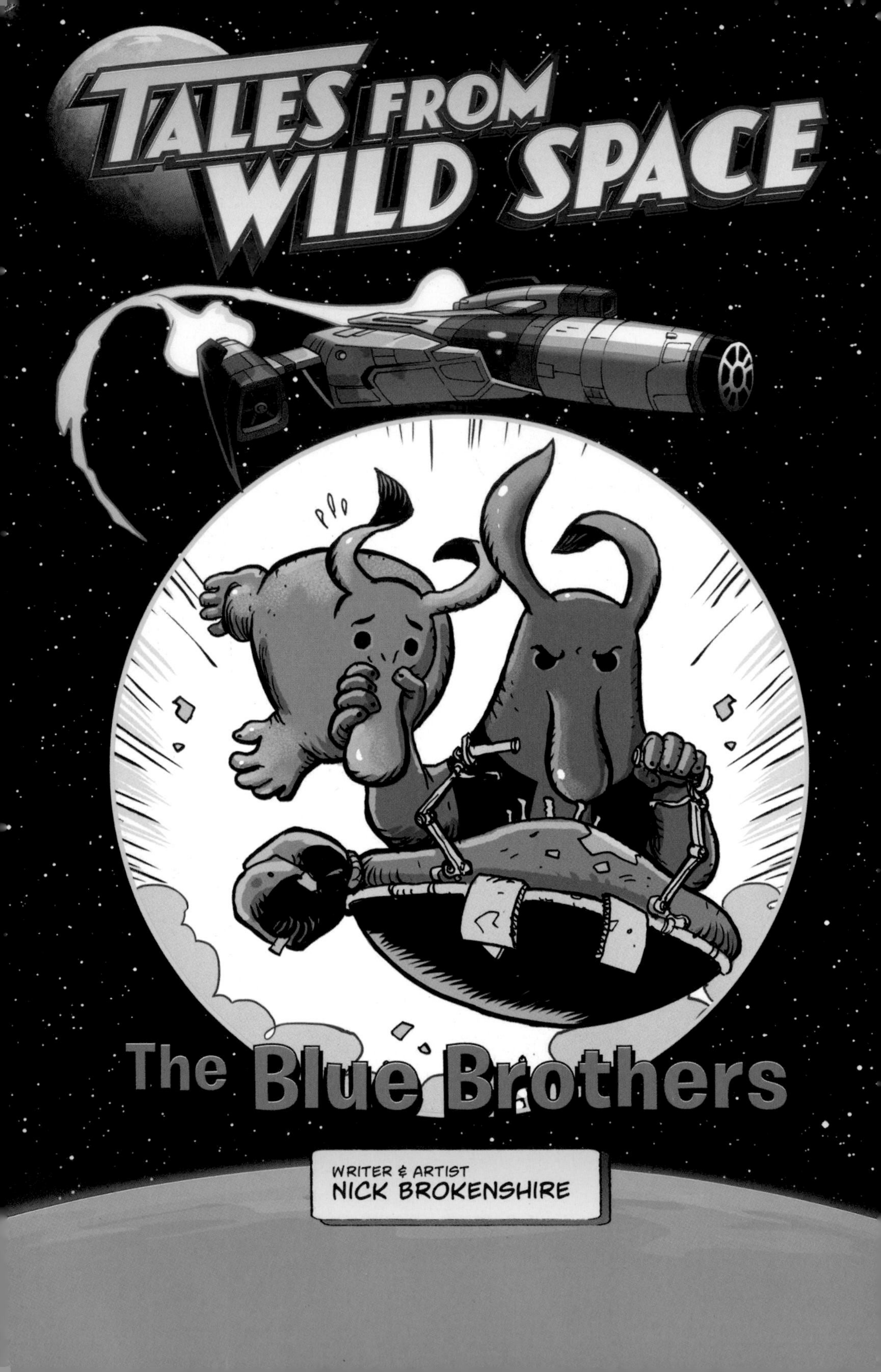
TALES FROM WILD SPACE
The Blue Brothers
WRITER & ARTIST
NICK BROKENSHIRE

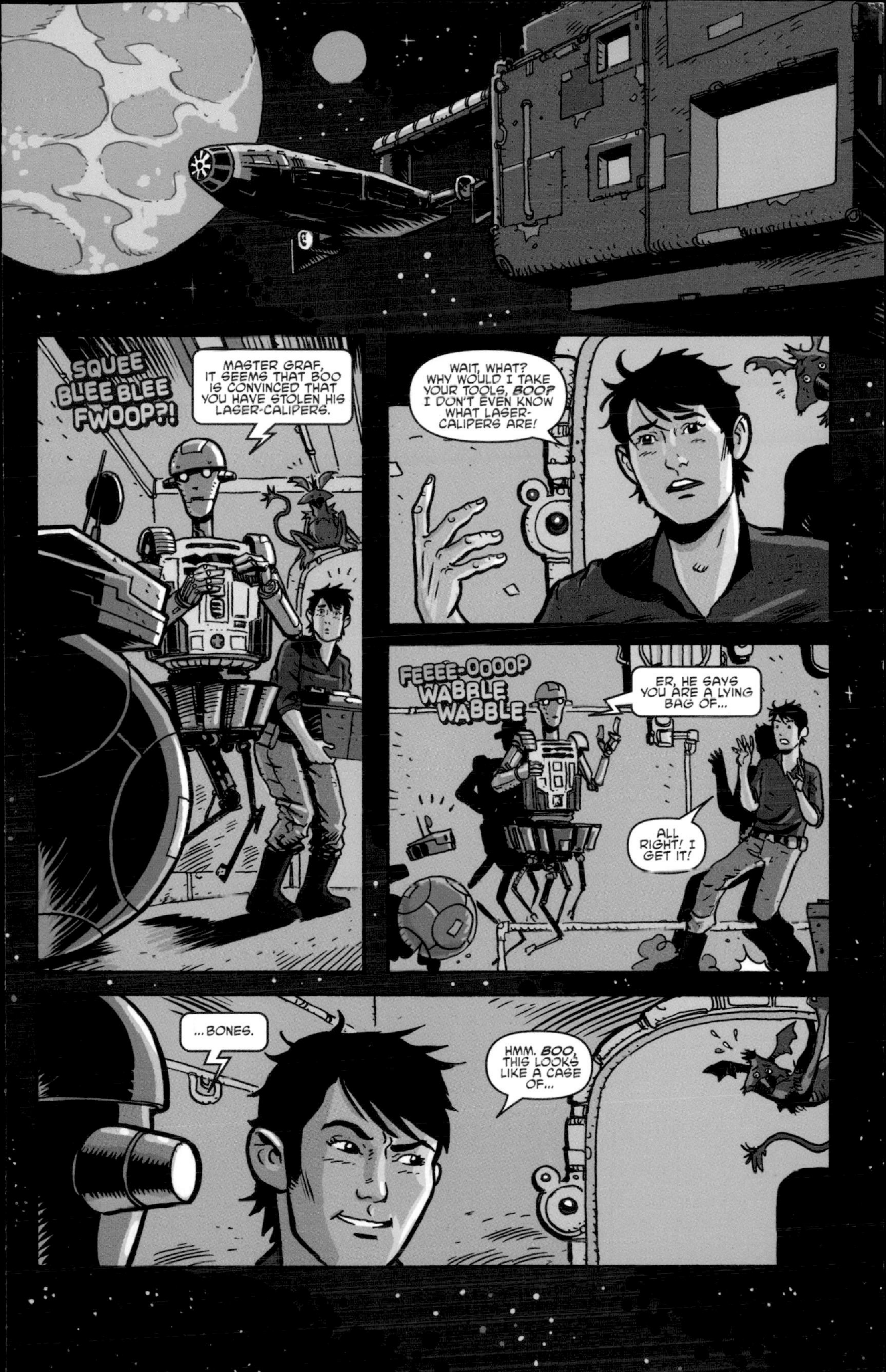
SQUEE BLEE BLEE FWOOP?!
MASTER GRAF, IT SEEMS THAT BOO IS CONVINCED THAT YOU HAVE STOLEN HIS LASER-CALIPERS.
WAIT, WHAT? WHY WOULD I TAKE YOUR TOOLS, BOO? I DON'T EVEN KNOW WHAT LASER-CALIPERS ARE!
FEEEE-OOOOP WABBLE WABBLE
ER, HE SAYS YOU ARE A LYING BAG OF...
ALL RIGHT! I GET IT!
...BONES.
HMM. BOO, THIS LOOKS LIKE A CASE OF...

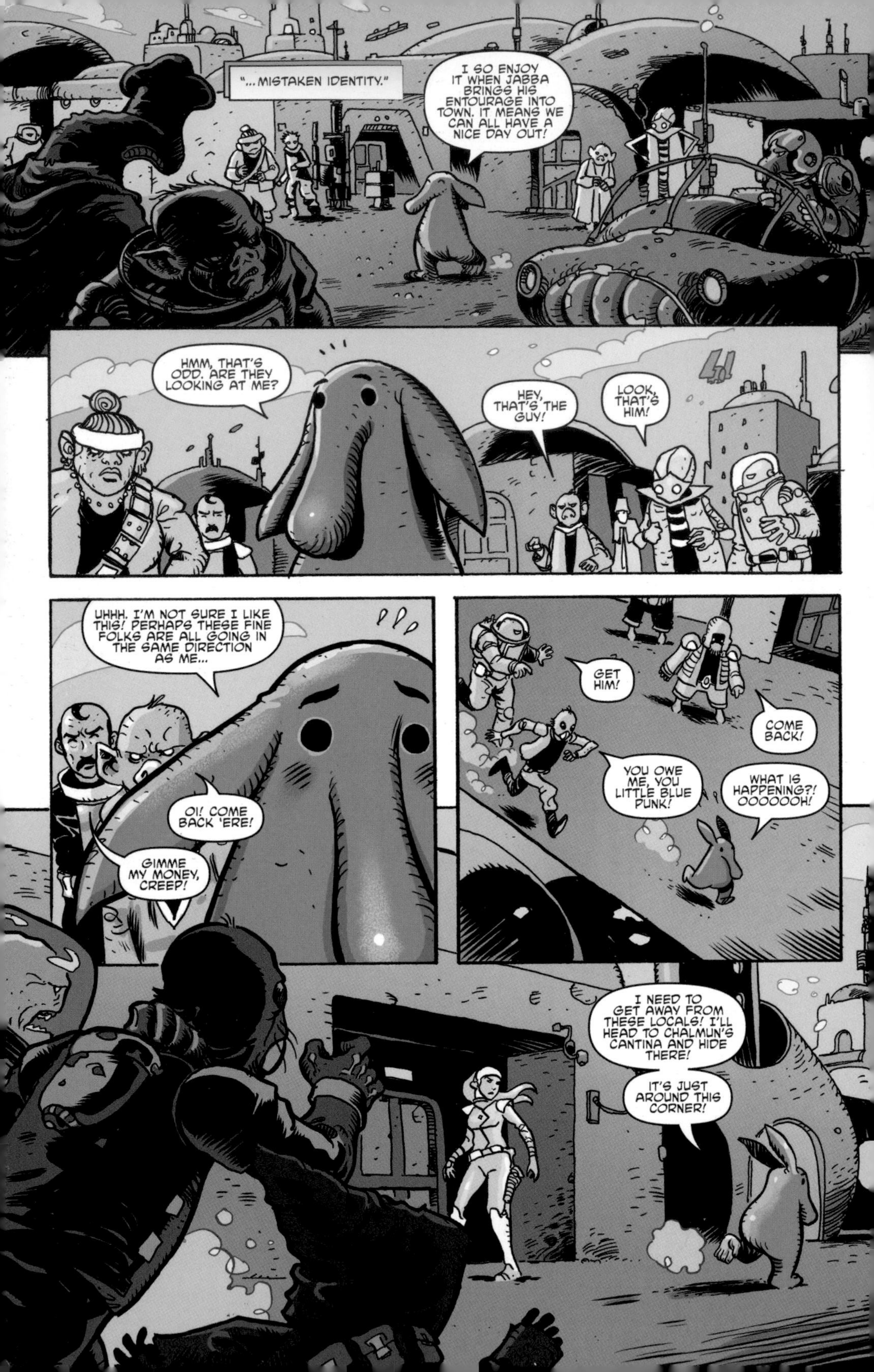
"...MISTAKEN IDENTITY."
I SO ENJOY IT WHEN JABBA BRINGS HIS ENTOURAGE INTO TOWN. IT MEANS WE CAN ALL HAVE A NICE DAY OUT!
HMM, THAT'S ODD. ARE THEY LOOKING AT ME?
HEY, THAT'S THE GUY!
LOOK, THAT'S HIM!
UHHH. I'M NOT SURE I LIKE THIS! PERHAPS THESE FINE FOLKS ARE ALL GOING IN THE SAME DIRECTION AS ME...
OI! COME BACK 'ERE!
GIMME MY MONEY, CREEP!
GET HIM!
COME BACK!
YOU OWE ME, YOU LITTLE BLUE PUNK!
WHAT IS HAPPENING?! OOOOOOH!
I NEED TO GET AWAY FROM THESE LOCALS! I'LL HEAD TO CHALMUN'S CANTINA AND HIDE THERE!
IT'S JUST AROUND THIS CORNER!

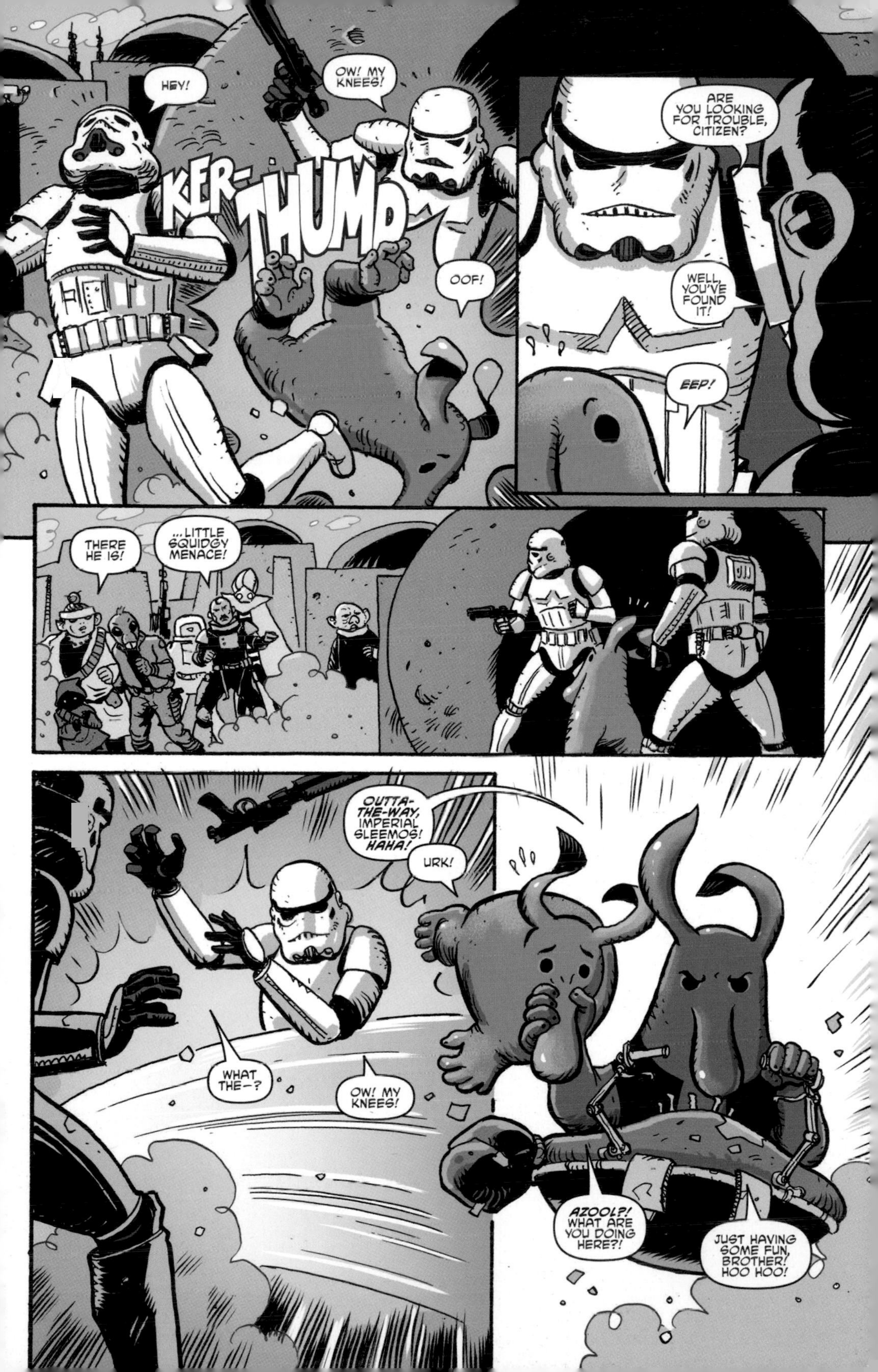
HEY!
OW! MY KNEES!
KER-THUMP
OOF!
ARE YOU LOOKING FOR TROUBLE, CITIZEN?
WELL, YOU'VE FOUND IT!
EEP!
THERE HE IS!
...LITTLE SQUIDGY MENACE!
OUTTA-THE-WAY, IMPERIAL SLEEMOS! HAHA!
URK!
WHAT THE-?
OW! MY KNEES!
AZOOL?! WHAT ARE YOU DOING HERE?!
JUST HAVING SOME FUN, BROTHER! HOO HOO!

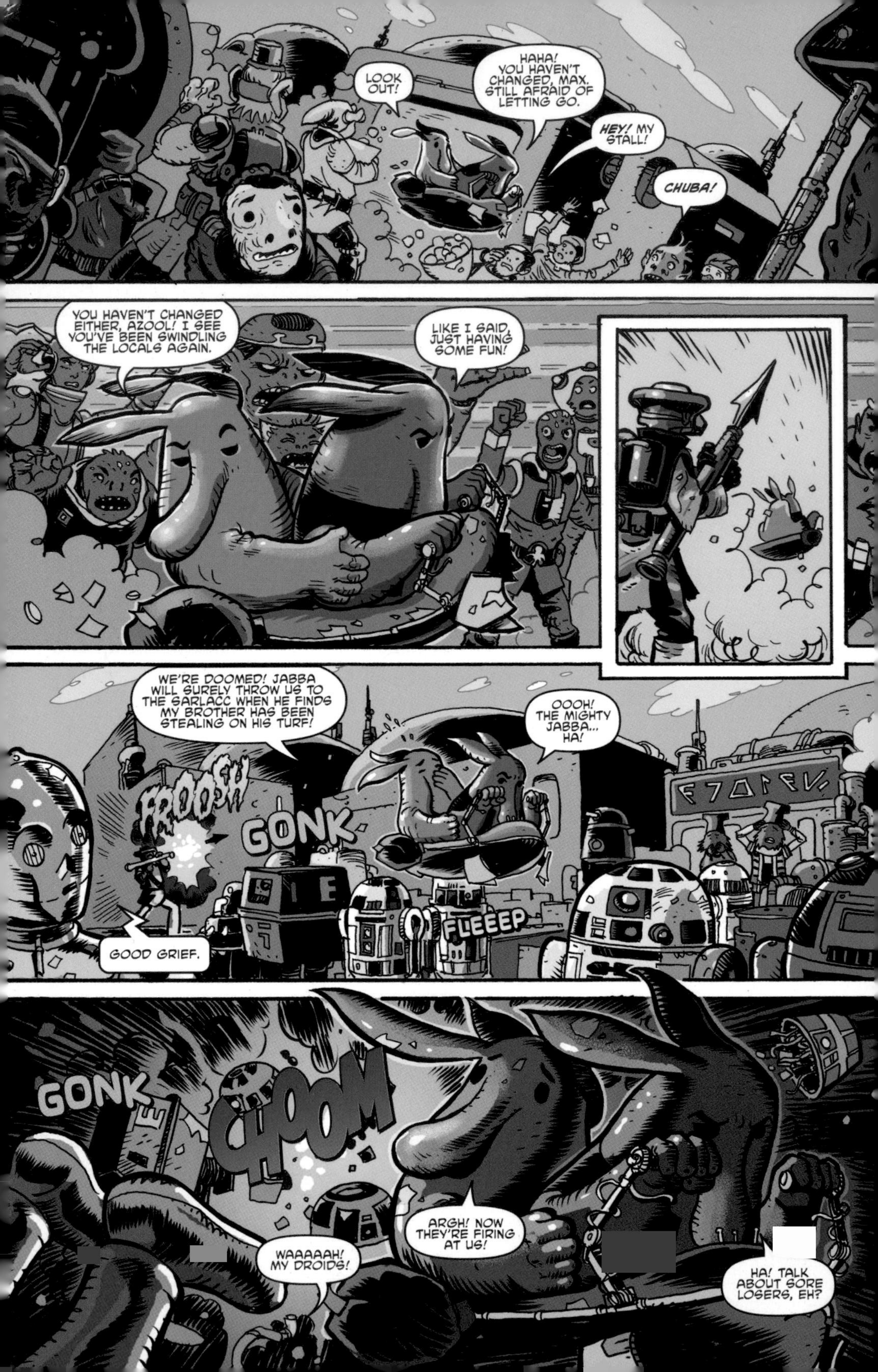
LOOK OUT!
HAHA! YOU HAVEN'T CHANGED, MAX. STILL AFRAID OF LETTING GO.
HEY! MY STALL!
CHUBA!
YOU HAVEN'T CHANGED EITHER, AZOOL! I SEE YOU'VE BEEN SWINDLING THE LOCALS AGAIN.
LIKE I SAID, JUST HAVING SOME FUN!
WE'RE DOOMED! JABBA WILL SURELY THROW US TO THE SARLACC WHEN HE FINDS MY BROTHER HAS BEEN STEALING ON HIS TURF!
OOOH! THE MIGHTY JABBA... HA!
FROOSH
GONK
FLEEEP
GOOD GRIEF.
GONK
CHOOM
WAAAAAH! MY DROIDS!
ARGH! NOW THEY'RE FIRING AT US!
HA! TALK ABOUT SORE LOSERS, EH?

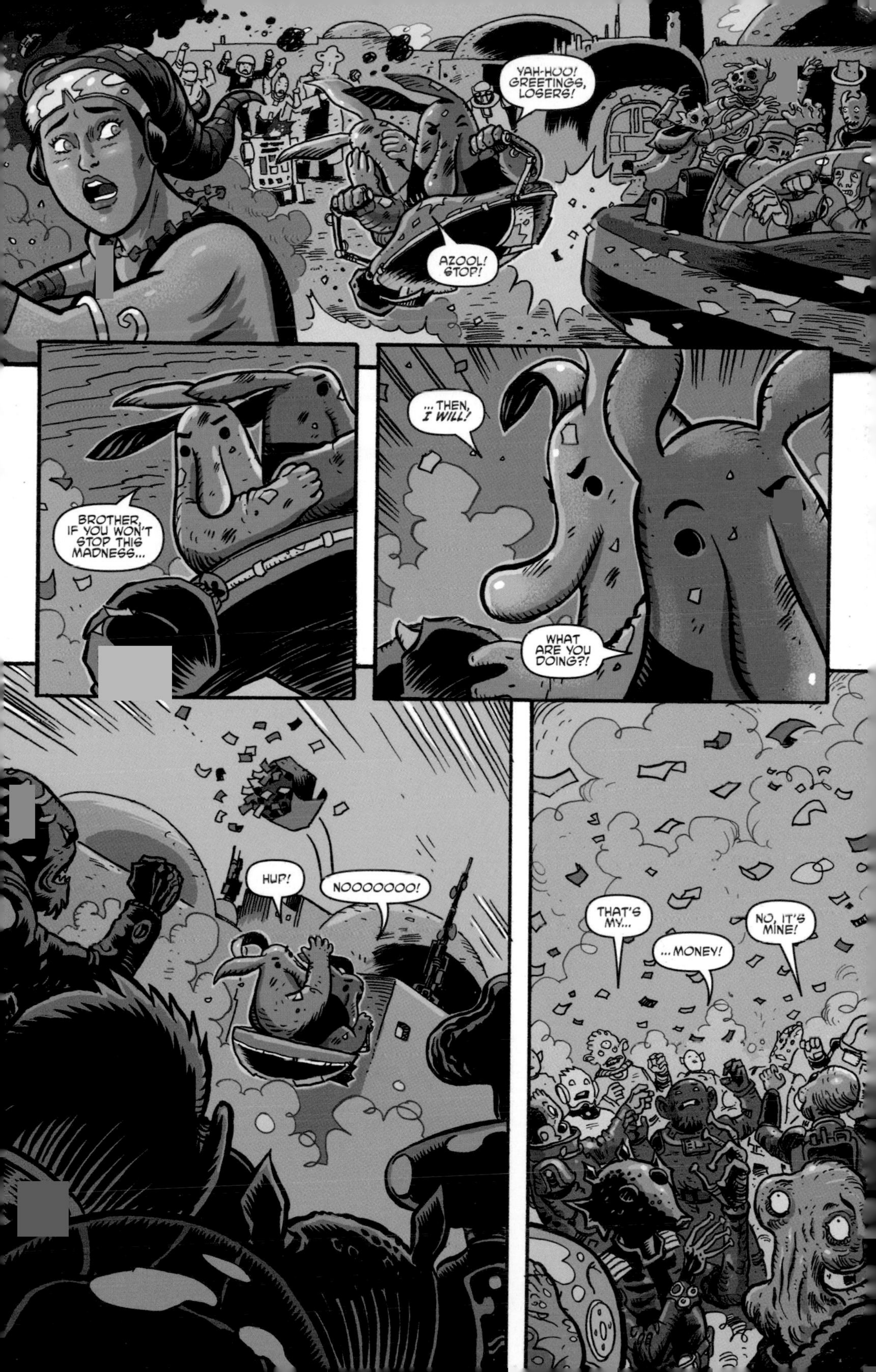
YAH-HOO! GREETINGS, LOSERS!
AZOOL! STOP!
BROTHER, IF YOU WON'T STOP THIS MADNESS...
...THEN, *I WILL!*
WHAT ARE YOU DOING?!
HUP!
NOOOOOOOO!
THAT'S MY...
...MONEY!
NO, IT'S MINE!

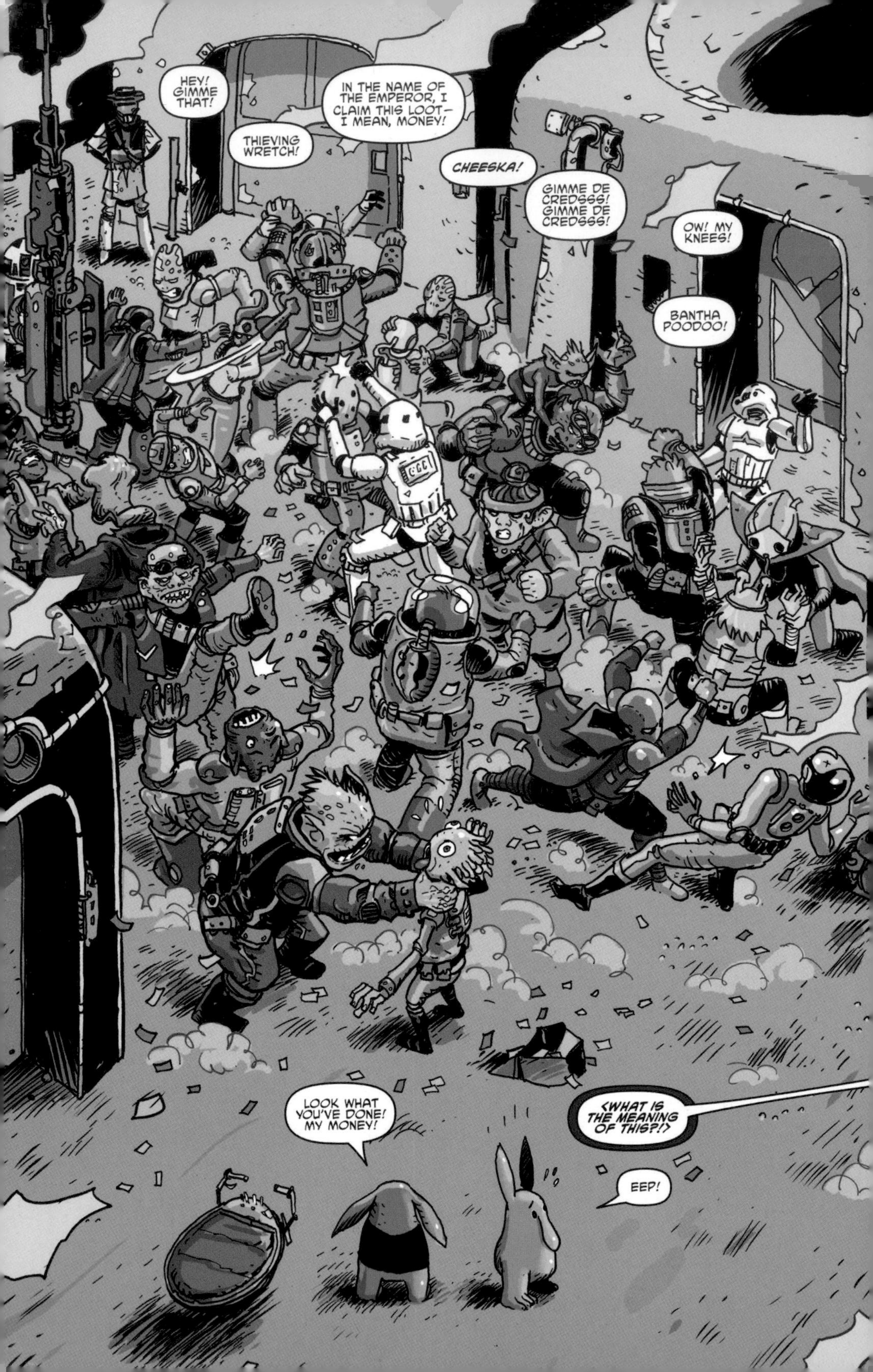
HEY! GIMME THAT!
THIEVING WRETCH!
IN THE NAME OF THE EMPEROR, I CLAIM THIS LOOT— I MEAN, MONEY!
CHEESKA!
GIMME DE CREDSSS! GIMME DE CREDSSS!
OW! MY KNEES!
BANTHA POODOO!
LOOK WHAT YOU'VE DONE! MY MONEY!
<WHAT IS THE MEANING OF THIS?!>
EEP!

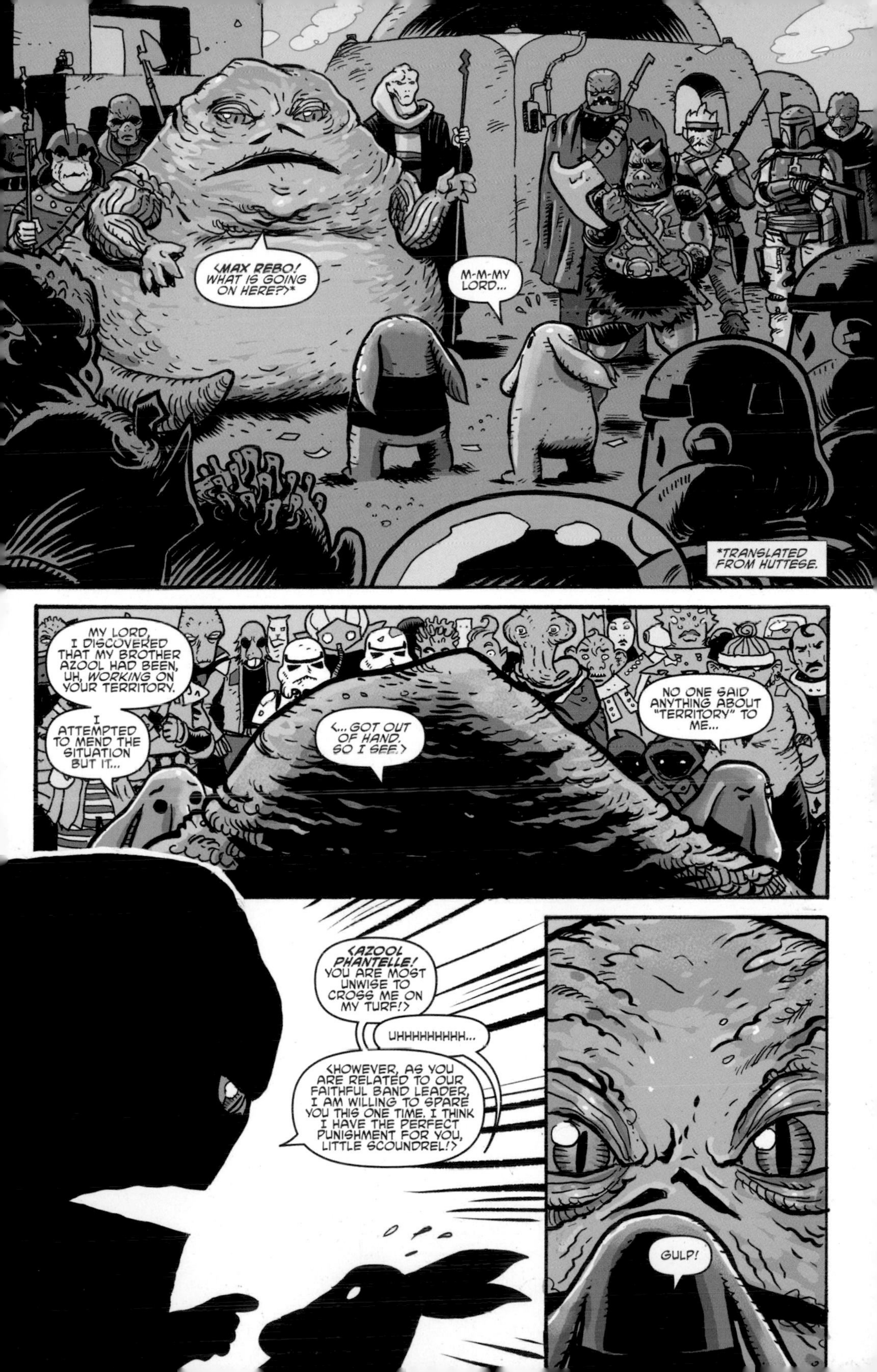

<MAX REBO! WHAT IS GOING ON HERE?>*
M-M-MY LORD...
*TRANSLATED FROM HUTTESE.
MY LORD, I DISCOVERED THAT MY BROTHER AZOOL HAD BEEN, UH, WORKING ON YOUR TERRITORY.
I ATTEMPTED TO MEND THE SITUATION BUT IT...
<...GOT OUT OF HAND. SO I SEE.>
NO ONE SAID ANYTHING ABOUT "TERRITORY" TO ME...
<AZOOL PHANTELLE! YOU ARE MOST UNWISE TO CROSS ME ON MY TURF!>
UHHHHHHHHHH...
<HOWEVER, AS YOU ARE RELATED TO OUR FAITHFUL BAND LEADER, I AM WILLING TO SPARE YOU THIS ONE TIME. I THINK I HAVE THE PERFECT PUNISHMENT FOR YOU, LITTLE SCOUNDREL!>
GULP!

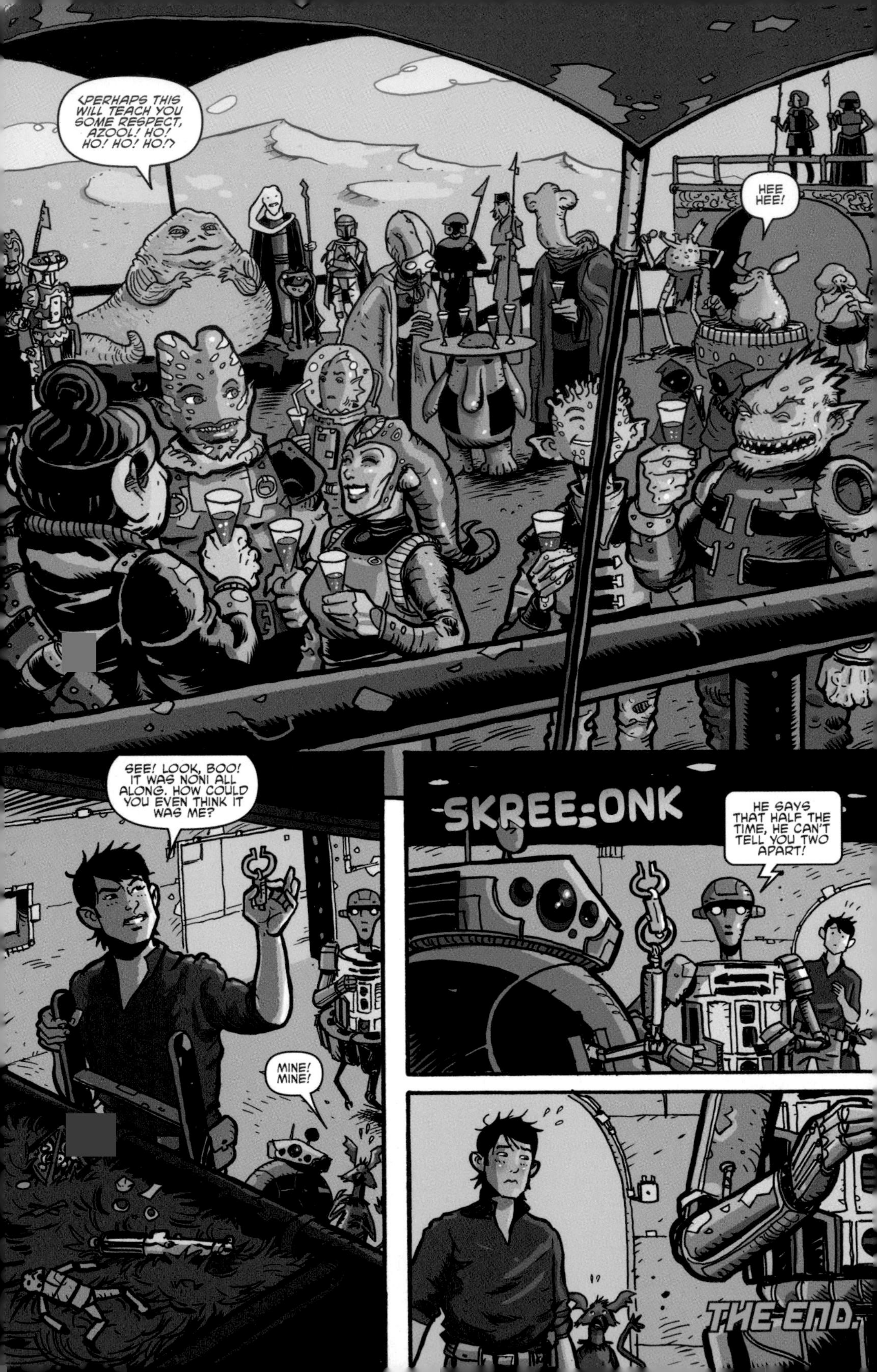
<PERHAPS THIS WILL TEACH YOU SOME RESPECT, AZOOL! HO! HO! HO! HO!>
HEE HEE!
SEE! LOOK, BOO! IT WAS NONI ALL ALONG. HOW COULD YOU EVEN THINK IT WAS ME?
MINE! MINE!
SKREE-ONK
HE SAYS THAT HALF THE TIME, HE CAN'T TELL YOU TWO APART!
THE END.

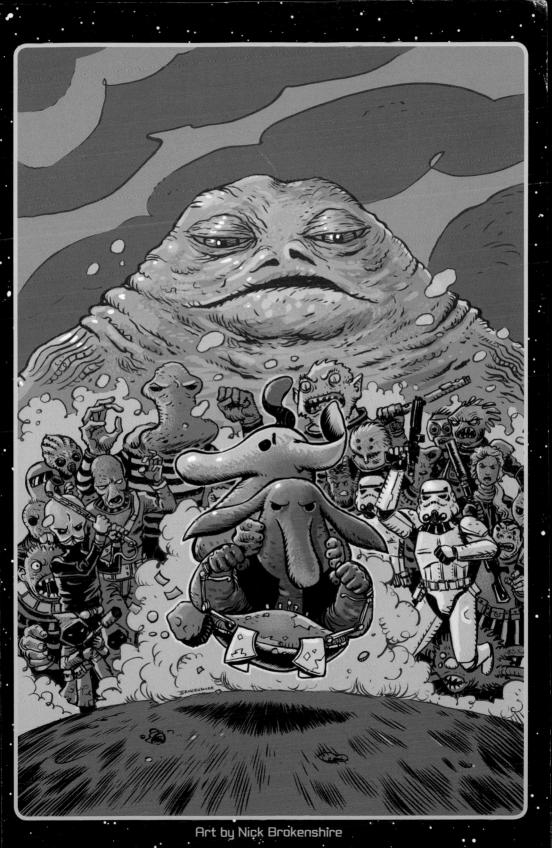

Art by Nick Brokenshire

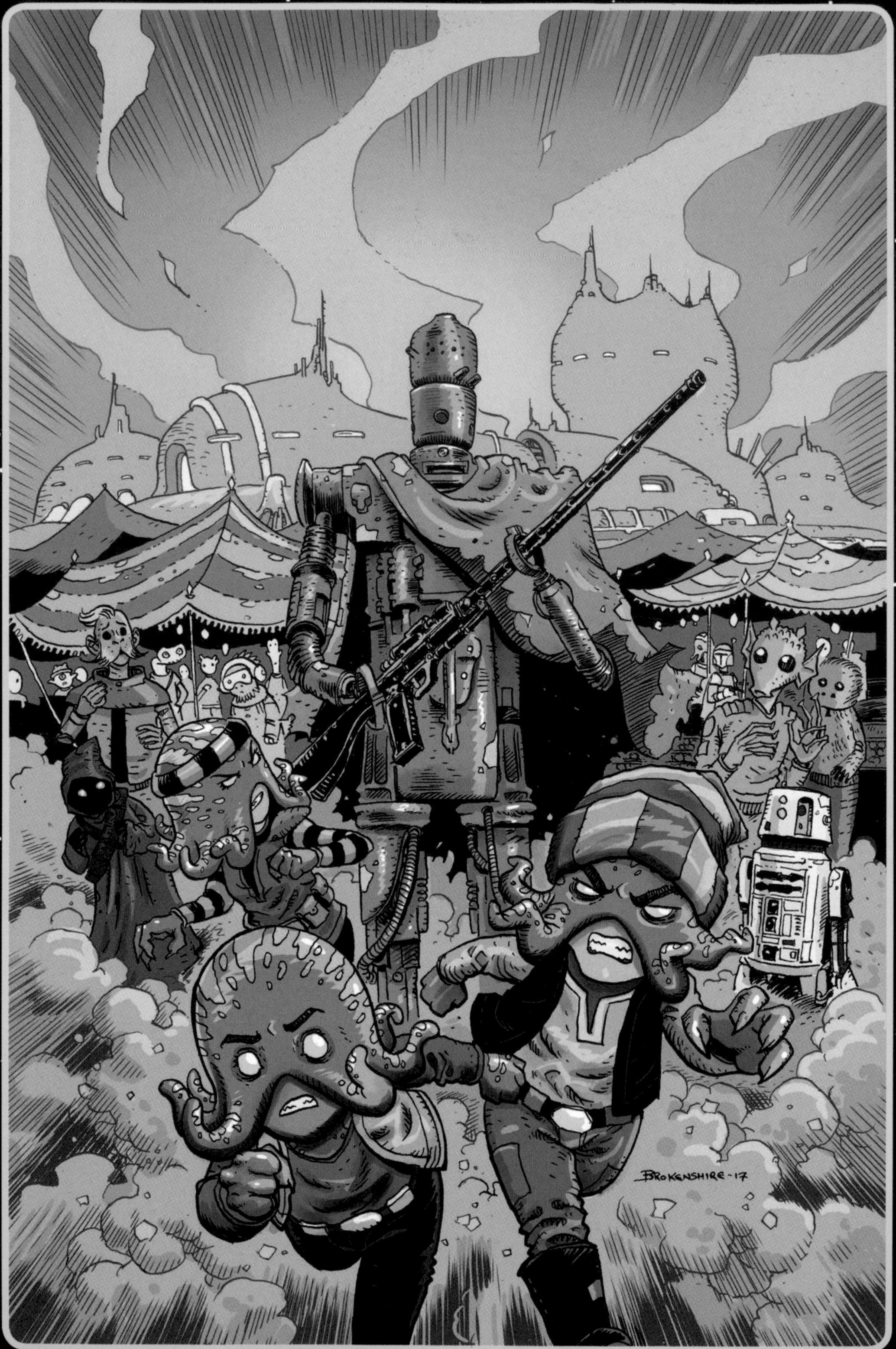
BROKENSHIRE-17

Art by Nick Brokenshire

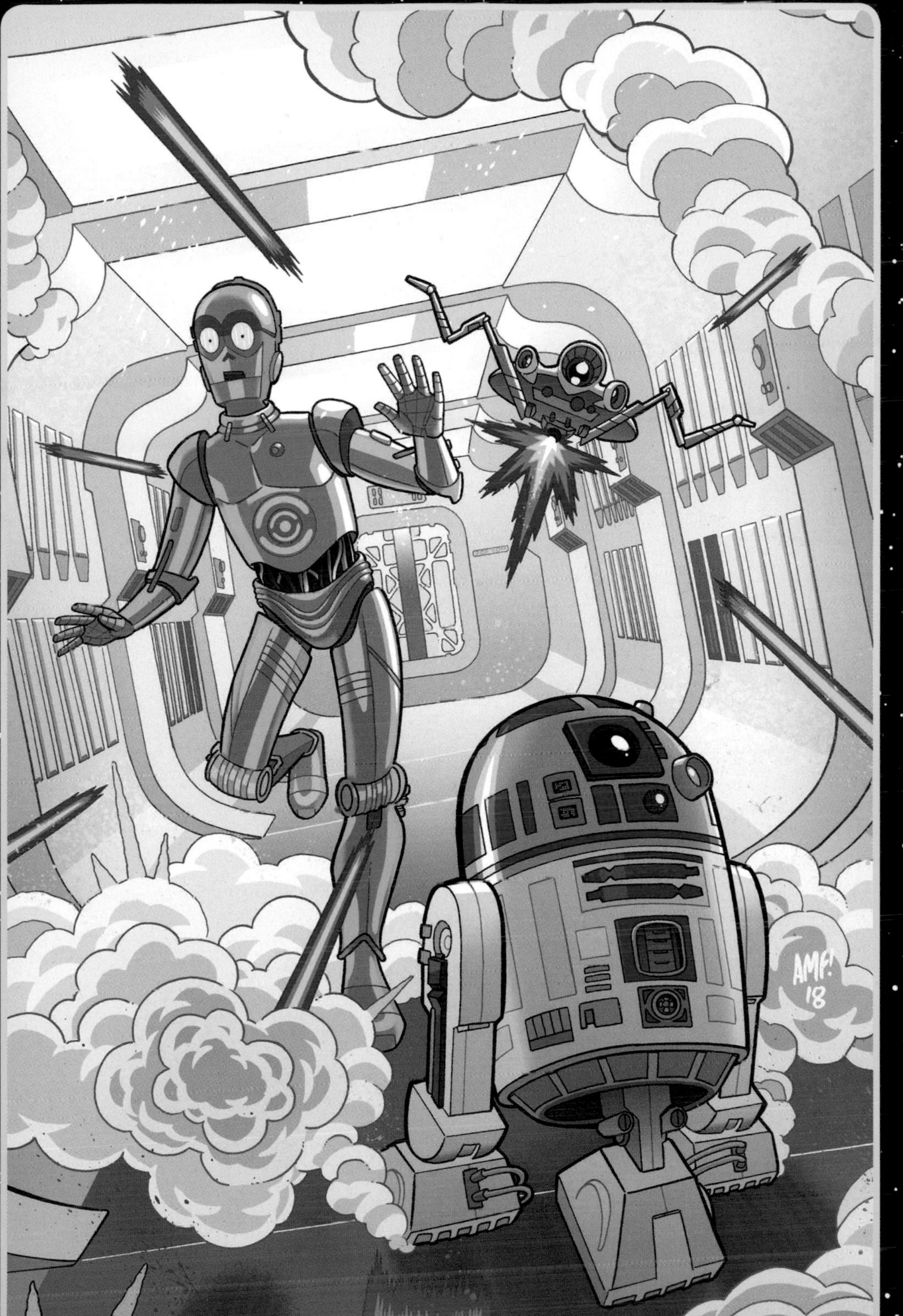
AMF!
'18

Art by Tony Fleecs

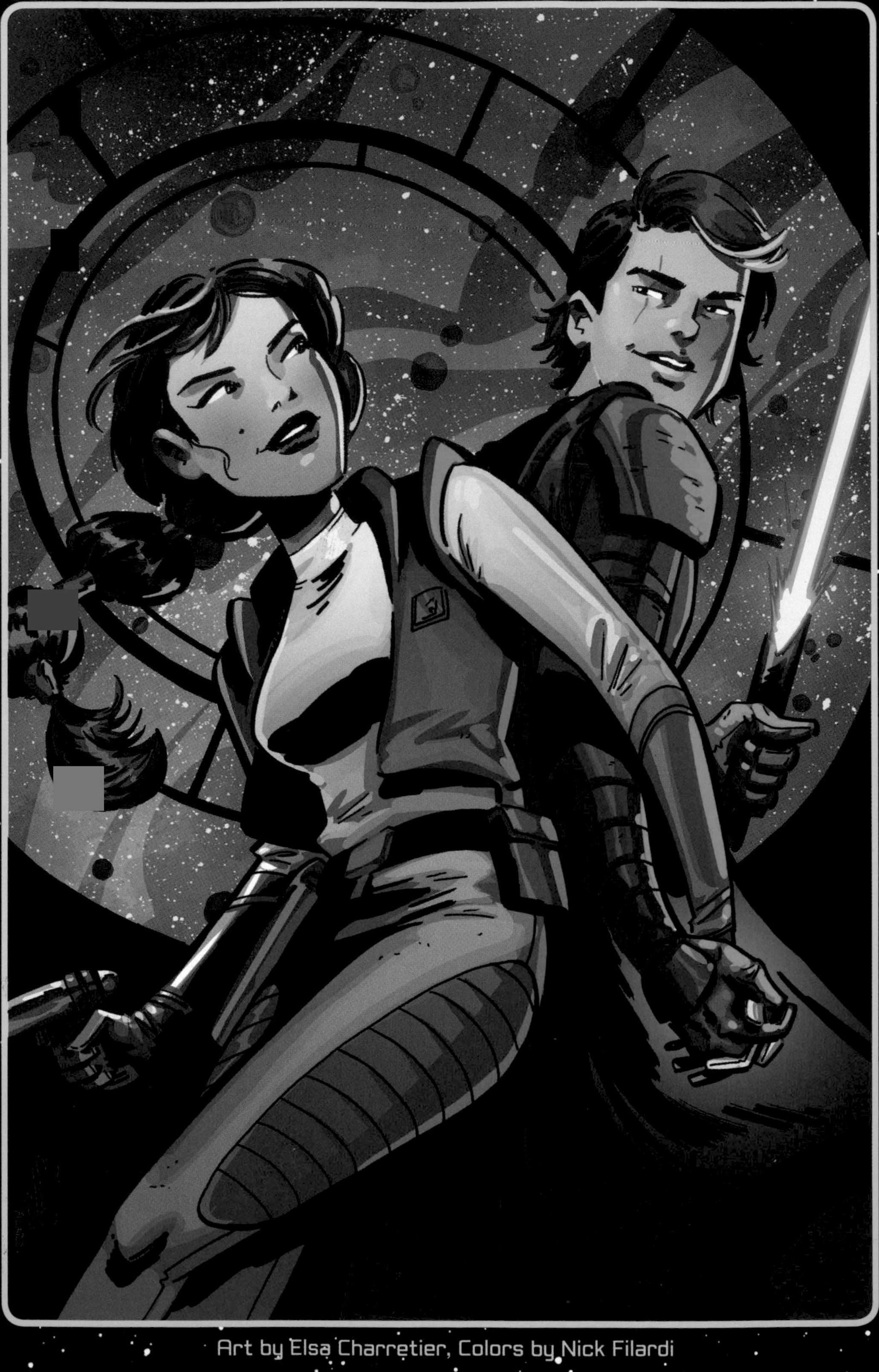

Art by Elsa Charretier, Colors by Nick Filardi

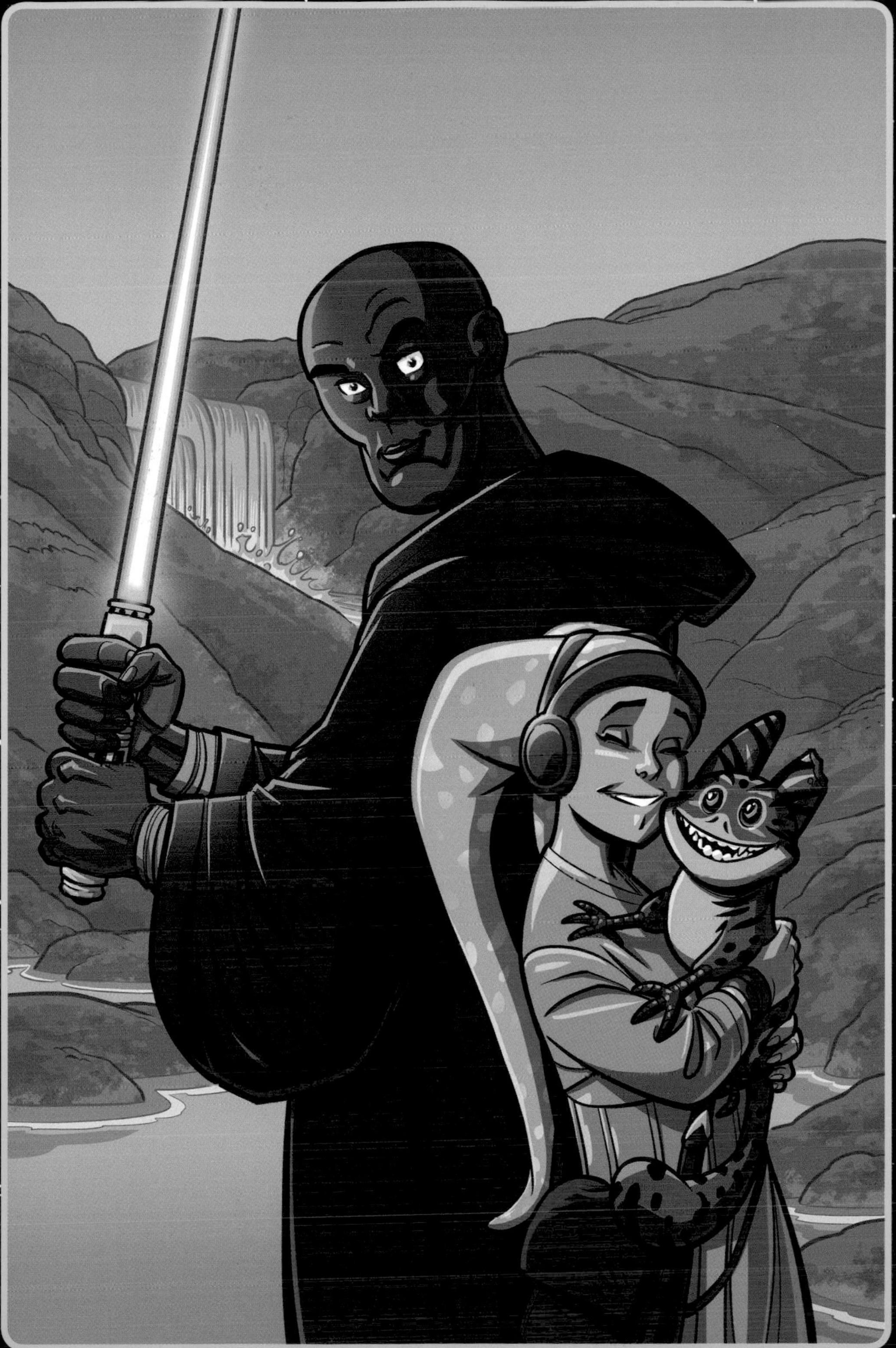

Art by Mauricet

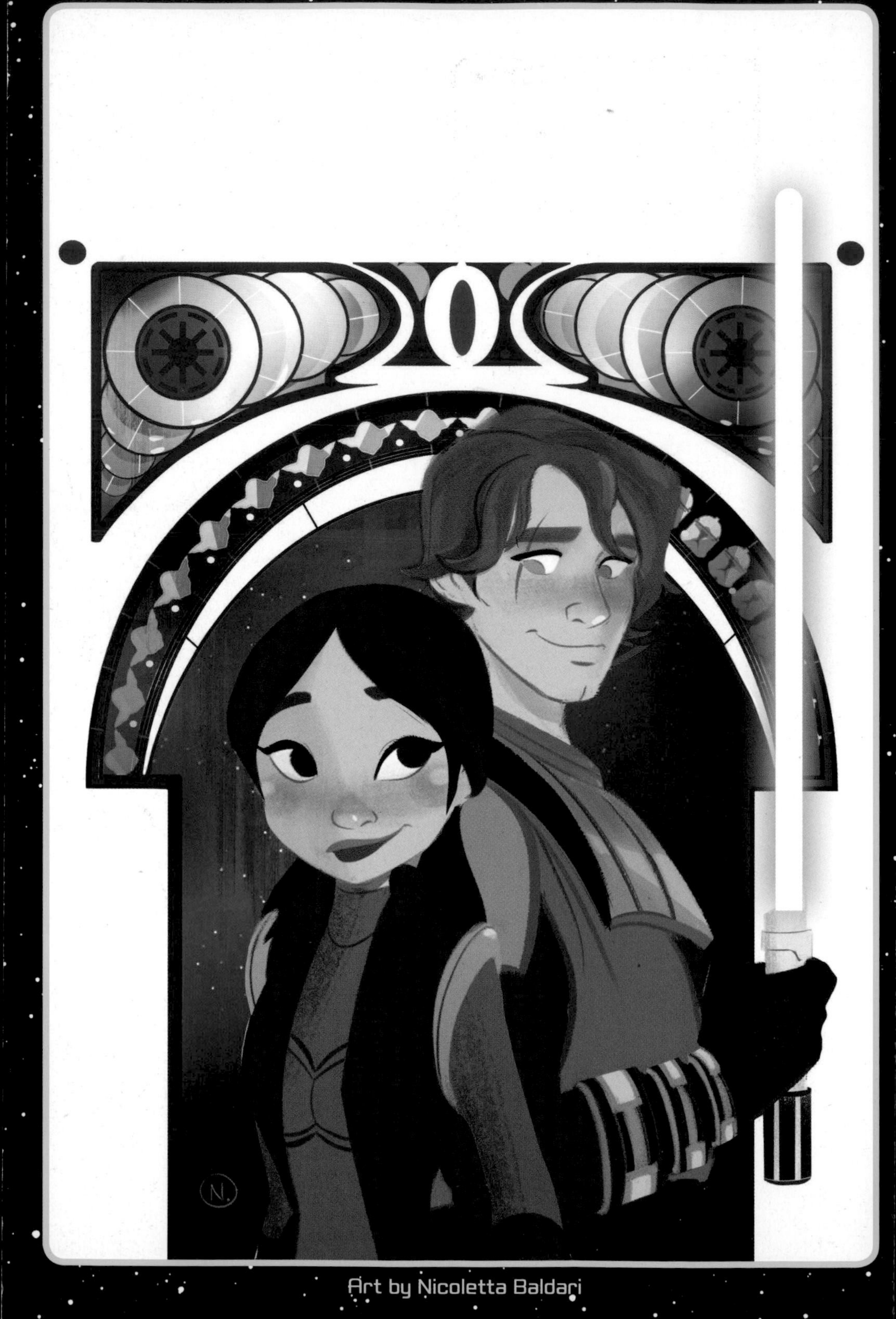

Art by Nicoletta Baldari

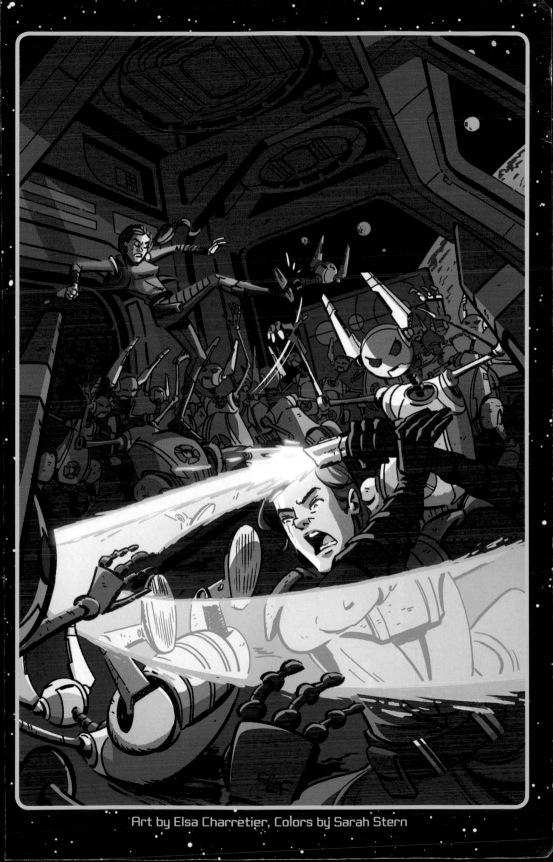

Art by Elsa Charretier, Colors by Sarah Stern

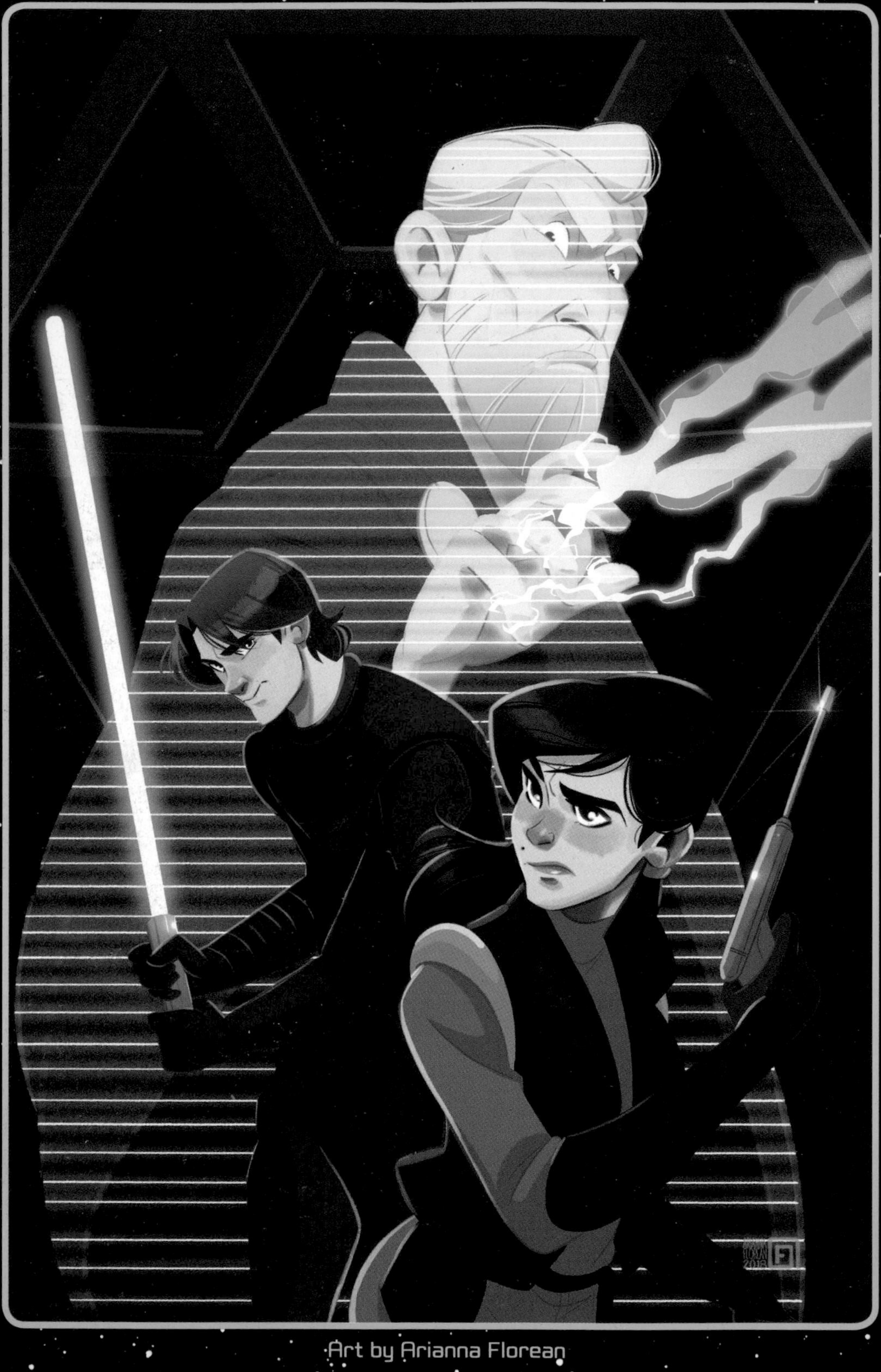

Art by Arianna Florean